# Haunted Hearts

## Teresa DesJardien

To Robin—
Appreciate your
work for the Board and
your insight!
Happy reading—
Teresa
DesJardien

Haunted Hearts / Teresa DesJardien. — 1st ed.
ISBN 978-0-9862126-2-8

*Dedication*

*Alice Brant and Ray Brant (1931-2008)*
*--a.k.a. Mom and Dad--*
*Thanks for arranging it so I could be*
*born on All Souls' Day.*

# Chapter 1

Olivia Beacham, the widowed Viscountess Stratton, looked out her bedchamber window at a drifting fog. "It's the perfect weather for tonight," she told her little dark-haired maid.

"'Tis the perfect night for finding trouble," Mary Kate countered.

"Oh," Olivia said fervently, "I do hope so."

Mary Kate, Irish Catholic, crossed herself and shook her head at her mistress. "Don't be tempting wicked things what are out and about on All Hallows Eve, m'lady."

Olivia took no offense at the warning nor did she scold the girl. Mary Kate had long since earned her loose tongue and the freedom of her Papist habits; the two of them were more friends than mistress and maid, no matter what the rest of the society would think of that.

Their need had been mutual: Olivia, so alone after so much death, the last being Stratton's; Mary Kate, adrift after her shop-owner parents had perished in a fire. Olivia had advertised for a maid, and Mary Kate had been the first to come, falling at Olivia's feet and weeping terribly while begging in her lilting accent for employment. No references. No experience. Any reasonable person would have turned her away without a second thought. Except, Olivia knew what it was to be an orphan, one who had the bare advantage of sometimes being remembered by her siblings, whereas Mary Kate had no-one. Olivia had hired her at once, and an irrevocable bond had been formed.

"Let me take down them two ruches on yer dress," Mary Kate tried one more time.

Olivia turned to look again into her long cheval glass. She tilted a leg and admired a shoe and inch of stocking made visible where the fabric had been hitched up with needle and thread. It *was* shocking.

That's why she shook her head. *I* want *to be daring.*

She reached for her mask. She'd bought it the day after she'd opened her invitation to a fancy dress party. It was to be a masquerade, to be thrown on and celebrating All Hallow's Eve, a pagan custom Londoners had centuries since foresworn.

Except for the black crepe hair-hood that would be pinned in place to cover her red-gold locks, raising the mask completed her costume. The mask was that of a cat: a black and white velvet cat's face, complete with ears, eyeholes, stiff little whiskers, and a delicate feline mouth, all of which obscured virtually all of Olivia's face. She watched her green eyes glitter back at her through the mask, the only facial feature that showed except a little bit of chin. The black and white spots of her mask were echoed by the colors of her skirts, along with a cloth cat's tail that trailed behind from her waist.

It was not the cat theme of the ensemble to which Mary Kate objected, but the daringly tight and low décolletage and the way Olivia had requested the layers of her skirts be caught up, the two ruches at either ankle, revealing those so-shocking glimpses of stocking and little black slippers.

"Yer look indecent," Mary Kate dared to say.

Olivia laughed instead of reprimanding. "I meant to."

"And yer should put yer wedding ring on again, m'lady."

Olivia looked down at her naked left hand and slowly shook her head. "I'm not married. My husband is dead."

Mary Kate sighed and tried a different tack. "There's plenty o' other events to start yer return into society. Yer don't need to be

6

going to some affair what's all about play-acting, and drinking too much, and who knows what manner of sinfulness--"

"I want some excitement," Olivia said, her voice so wistful it made her servant fall quiet and bite her lip. "I've been in mourning for four years. Four years! First Papa passed, then Mama, and then Stratton." She'd never gotten used to calling her ancient husband by his Christian name, Robert. "I'm only four-and-twenty! I spent two years married to an old man who never danced, nor dined out, nor freely welcomed callers. He all but slept 'round the clock in his final months. Since I agreed to accept Stratton's hand I've only ever gone to two parties, and one of those was the wedding."

Olivia knew she was being ungrateful. Lord Stratton had given her a home, a respectable reputation, security, and had kept her from being too much alone, even if their life together had been dull, dull, dull. He'd even, to a lesser degree, satisfied her unspoken curiosity about men's bodies. It wasn't his fault she'd never come to love him--although it was his doing that she'd not even come to like him much.

Mary Kate's eyes suddenly brimmed with tears. The maid knew how lonely her mistress was. She was the one person in this world Olivia was sure loved her--and the fierce little dragon knew she could say most anything she felt needed saying. "But yer mourning ain't over for two more months!"

"Pish."

"Some people mind such details."

Olivia gave a little shoulder shrug. "All the more reason to attend a fancy dress party. I won't remove my mask. I'll leave before midnight, when they're traditionally doffed. No one will ever know the Widow Stratton was there--if they even have a thought to spare for me." *Which I doubt. In terms of eligibility or desirability or visibility, in the eyes of the ton, I'm completely forgotten.*

"What if someone recognizes yer voice? One of yer church or reading society ladies?"

Olivia smiled, liking her ready answer. "I speak creditable French. I shall put on ze accent," the last sentence was inflected to demonstrate the effect.

Mary Kate seemed poised to argue further, but instead she sighed and her tensed shoulders fell; Olivia had won. That'd been how things were going to end anyway, but the small triumph only lent itself to Olivia's growing giddiness. *I am going to a party! I am going to laugh, and flirt, and dance.*

She put aside her mask to reach for a small purse. Taking that and Mary Kate's hand, she pulled her maid to the second of two wardrobes. Opening the doors one at a time, she pointed to all the gowns hanging on their pegs. "Take those, all of them, and this." She pressed the purse into Mary Kate's hands. "Buy some packets of dye. All of these gray and lavender gowns are yours now. Dye them to happier colors, if you please. And cut up the black ones, or offer them for charity, or do what you will with them."

"Those're fine materials, those black ones. Surely yer want to keep at least one? Yer never knows--"

Olivia firmly shook her head, lips thinned out. "No more black. No more funerals or mourning. Not for me."

The maid would have refused such a bounty, probably, if she hadn't been aware of all the new dresses hanging in the second wardrobe. Gowns of gold and green and blue, designs more dashing than anything Olivia had worn since the two of them had met.

"Can I share 'em with Ginnie and Anna?" Mary Kate asked, referring to the other household maids, her eyes beginning to glitter with the thought of new gowns.

"Of course you may," Olivia said. "And make use of anything you find in the linen cupboard. Buttons, and ribbons, and such."

"Oh, thank you, m'lady!" Mary Kate lifted both hands, the purse clasped between her fingers. A grin of pure pleasure grew on her face--until another glance at her mistress's masquerade garb made sure it

8

was not long-lived. She narrowed her eyes. "I still think them ruches
of yers oughta come down. It'd take me but a moment--"

Olivia laughed and swept up the mask with its hood she and
Mary Kate had designed between them. "No, dear girl. It's time to
tie this in place. My wicked masquerade awaits."

***

The intrigue of her disguise, the efforts at concealment, only
added to Olivia's growing excitement as her carriage neared the
house of her All Hallows party host. Lord Quinn was a man whose
interests caused whispers to float even to the ears of a woman who
spent too much time alone--a titillating reputation that had only
added to Olivia's determination to finally break her soul-stifling
mourning early.

When the carriage rolled to a stop, she took as deep a breath as
her tight and low bodice would permit before she allowed the
footman to hand her down. Even though she longed to expand her
very narrow world, it had been a long time since she'd faced the
prying eyes of greater society, even if they could only guess who she
was behind her mask.

Still, Olivia began to all but float, her own daring--*finally, finally
daring to be free!*--buoying her as she stepped up the stairs to the
house, the night air cool where her bits of stocking peeked out from
among her skirts. With every new moment of liberty she grew more
and more giddy. Unfettered laughter, the kind that had made many
scoldings come her way as a child, threatened to burst from her lips
any moment. A sparkling sensation, not unlike champagne, ran
through her blood. It raced into her limbs, giving her posture--had
she but known it--a cavalier air that drew the eye.

As soon as she was inside, she whisked off her pelisse and
relinquished it to a servant. Exposing her bodice's bounty was
rewarded by a lifting of the footman's brows before he bowed her
toward the butler. Even the butler, stiff with his stoic duties and

9

obvious years of service, allowed one blink as she approached. Her hands did not rise to tug her bodice up, even though the impulse flickered for a moment. She had to suppress another impulse to giggle. Falling into line behind a man and woman who were dressed as Poseidon and Aphrodite, she observed that their clothes shimmered, and their inadequate masks revealed here was Lady Bettonstone and presumably her husband.

No names were announced and the invitation vellums were dropped into a lidded box after being glanced at, but the butler did strike a long staff upon the tiles with the entry of each arrival. Thus announced without a word, Olivia moved into the crowd. Since she had purposely arrived late, her host--a man she'd met exactly once at her home, when Stratton was yet alive--was no longer in position near the door as he would have been to greet his more timely guests.

She was instantly pleased by the crush, for it took her only a fleeting minute to feel as though she had blended into the throng of masked humanity around her.

Almost everyone was in costume--with the exception of a few ancients who, one must assume, decried such folderol--and it made an already unusual night seem all the more so by the variety and splendor of the costumes all around her. There were knights and damsels, kings and queens, devils and angels, pirates, conquistadors, Greeks and Romans, and quite some few rams and bulls. The ladies had chosen to dress as a butterfly, or fairy, or a simple goose girl, but nearly all wore sparkling gems in their hair, on their wrists, or gracing their throats. The styles of masks ran from just a bit of kohl sketched about the eyes all the way to complete headpieces, one fellow sporting a whole unicorn's head, complete with a two-foot-long horn he seemed inclined to use with suggestive gestures.

On the other hand, there was a rather shocking lack of costume on some people, and other ensembles Olivia would never have donned no matter how much she longed to embrace one night with fewer rules. A man was dressed as a mummy, but his "wrappings" owed more to whitewash than to any coverings. Good heavens, was that his *navel?*

She turned quickly away--then slowly made herself turn around. She gave a tiny laugh, seeing that the navel had been painted in place atop some wrappings. But still...how to feel about such an immodest image, however false?

At last she did turn away, quite sure her cheeks were pink...and found she faced a long table groaning under an excess weight of elaborate flower arrangements and dozens of delicious-looking foodstuffs. Here was a roasted suckling pig, and there a plate of glistening oysters, buns savory and sweet, slices of squab in gravy, three tureens of fragrant soups, also nuts, sweetmeats, a quivering blanc mange, and so much more. The table was actually bowing under its bounty and flowery décor. It was overwhelming. Enticing. Bordering on sybaritic excess. It was only food...but still it gave Olivia the very kind of shiver she'd hoped to feel tonight.

A lady never over-sampled... But tonight she was no lady. Tonight she was a cat who would sample whatever took her fancy, and she would savor the indulgence until her tight bodice let her take no more.

Her filled plate was soon joined by a glass of sparkling wine she took from a footman's tray. After a moment, she had to laugh at herself, because of course her mask made consumption difficult. She found a corner with a niche where she balanced her plate, and fed herself morsels with one hand sneaking under the mask's edge that sat under her lower lip.

Perhaps too soon for her physical appetite--but not so for cravings after merriment and diversion--she abandoned her supper and the corner. Moving out among the throng, wine in hand even though she'd have a hard time sipping at it, Olivia circled slowly, looking for her night's fulfillment, whatever it would prove to be.

Musicians played quietly from behind a large screen, their gentle tunes sometimes all but lost under the conversation of the many guests. Candles flickered in the chandeliers overhead and all around the room, raising the temperature enough that garden doors had been thrown open against the heat of the lighting and the crowd.

A woman covered in feathers--a nightingale?--threw back her head and laughed unusually loudly at something said in the group around her, not the polite titter Olivia was used to among her small circle of ladies. *Would I dare copy her?* she mused.

There was a man in pirate costume, sweeping a lady milkmaid through the opened doors, out into the garden. He was laughing, and the woman was blushing but not pulling back against his leading hand.

"Meow," a man in a harlequin's suit said as he swept by, grabbing Olivia's attention. He stumbled, clearly already inebriated. Olivia began to bristle...but realized calls and trysts and a stranger's masked stare, indeed everything tonight was exactly the mischief for which she'd asked.

"Meow," she said back, smiling wide enough for the harlequin to see her lower teeth. She avoided his suddenly outstretched hand, laughing as she plunged away from him, not so much from being unsettled as from playing the coquette.

She floated among the crowd until she was sure the harlequin did not try to follow. She listened to this conversation for a while, then passed on to that one. People made room for her, and now and again a comment was thrown her way, but she merely murmured short, French-accented answers. The subject matters were plentiful, from governmental questions to latest fashions to sharp-tongued gossip. Dazzled by the others' quickness of thought or strong opinions, Olivia contributed little. Wine in one hand, she'd brought the cloth tail around from behind, and swung it idly as she moved from group to group.

Eventually a man in a half-mask and a domino longer and more flowing than her own modified version asked, "Half the fun is guessing who people are under their masks, eh? But who are you? I declare m'self stumped."

"I am only a *petit chat*," she answered.

He eyed her pointy-eared mask and her tail. "I can see that, but who are you really?"

"I cannot tell."

He pouted. "Well, I'm sure we'll all remove our masks at some point. I'll find out then, won't I?"

She only laughed for an answer, thinking she would not be here for him to see. But the time of any unmasking had not yet been announced, the likely time of midnight was a long way off, and so she would enjoy herself for the time being.

She let her pleasure build, cherishing the ability to go and do as she pleased. She occasionally smuggled more tidbits from trays and tables about the room up under her mask, and managed to find enough unviewed moments to lift her mask a little and sip at her refilled wine. She admired the house's lush boughs and sprays of cornstalks, apples, nuts, and a plethora of other harvest crops cleverly formed into table and wall decorations, noting the proverbial pineapples, obviously grown in some hothouse, that symbolized hospitality. All the while she laughed when something amused her, which was often. She felt a little light-headed from the wine, but also from the freedom and gaiety she'd made possible with her own actions.

Olivia spoke in her foreign tones for several minutes with an unknown Robin Hood. Like many of the guests, he was rather in his cups, but trying to be gallant.

"I say, you're very pretty," he slurred, standing closer than she was used to. She allowed this, just because it was rather daring to do so.

"But 'ow can you say zat? You cannot see my face."

"You have pretty light eyes, I can see them. What color is that? Green?"

"Blue," she fibbed, just to see if he challenged her.

"Ah, blue. Yes. So, you see, you are very pretty. Blue eyes are always very pretty."

He made her laugh twice before she bid him *adieu*, giving him a little wave with the end of her tail. Ignoring his protest, she moved to join a circle of ladies whom she discovered were doing their best to guess who their true love was to be. It was an old countrified custom wherein one pared a pippin, trying to remove the peel in one long continuous piece. The apple peel was then swung over the head three times, and tossed over the left shoulder. One lady gave a high-pitched squeal, claiming her peel had fallen into the shape of a G.

"Gordon," Olivia offered with a French pronunciation. "Or Georges."

"Ew!" said the pippin-tosser. "You cannot mean George Laskin?"

The other lady who had just tossed a pippin skin of her own said, "It doesn't count anyway. Your peel was broken. But look, mine isn't. I got a C."

This led to a good-natured argument between the two, from which Olivia turned to see two other ladies, their heads leaned back and their faces twitching awkwardly as they strove to dislodge one of the two apple seeds they'd each placed atop either eyelid. Inquiry supplied that each seed had been named for a different desired sweetheart. Other observers laughed or called out advice as the ladies strove to see that their preferred gentleman's namesake stayed in place while the less favored became the first seed to fall.

Another glance around the large room showed there were other such goings-on. How oddly charming. These were old games, some might even say servants's foolishness, but these were a bit of sport the masters had chosen to play.

14

"What a strange party," Olivia said under her breath, then giggled that she was present to see it for herself. Such curious sport, and attire, and behaviors. It was all more than she'd hoped for, on this night of her coming out anew.

She sauntered to an area where a lively set of gentlemen cried out comments as three others played snap apple, the latter leaping at some of the apples hanging from cords suspended from an overhead beam.

"Wait until it stops swinging!"

"No, you'll just set it to swinging again. Stand in front of it, let it come to you," Mr. Harrow, whom Olivia knew from church, advised. His sheep's mask was in his hand, and perhaps the red mark on his chin suggested he'd already had an unfortunate turn at the game himself.

"I'll take it in the eye!" protested his friend.

The three gentlemen were having very little luck achieving their goal of a bite, but perhaps that was because legend had it that the first to take a bite would be the first to marry. Olivia thought to join the raucous game--not that she had any plan of marrying again--but of course her mask would not allow it. After a time she wandered away, her smiling lips all but unseen behind the cat's mask.

There was a young couple, openly kissing. Now, truly, that was too much. Olivia would never have let Stratton kiss her in public; indeed, she'd avoided as many kisses as she could from her aged husband. All the same, her gaze sneaked back to the couple, and she tried to imagine actually enjoying a kiss, as they clearly did. *Will I ever?*

Sighing, she turned to spy her host. He was the center of a great deal of attention. Deservedly so, for his costume was splendid-- though unsettling. He wore no mask. He had no coat--Olivia had only ever seen a man without a coat when she'd gone to bed with her husband or seen laborers in the fields. Lord Quinn wore a shirt, if one could call the very thin lawn construction a shirt, and anyway it was unbuttoned all the way down to where it met his costume. He wore no cravat, his throat shockingly exposed. There were two horns, short like a nanny goat's, fixed in his dark hair. His lower limbs were covered with a suit sewn of variegated fur that might actually be from a goat, the creature he resembled. Well, "covered" was too generous a word: his calves and feet were bare--*bare!*--and there was but one angled strap of fur over his left shoulder and the shirt--and when he moved just so, his right nipple peeped through the ridiculously sheer fabric.

Olivia stared, appalled and fascinated.

For just a moment, in the flickers cast down from the chandelier above Lord Quinn, Olivia wondered if perhaps this was a truer image of the man and less a costume? He stood so...blatantly. So unashamed. Around the loins of this remarkable ensemble were cleverly draped and sewn fabrics fashioned to look like twining ivy and oak leaves. For a moment she named him a satyr, but then she shook her head, realizing he was--as evidenced from the smiling figure that had bedecked her invitation vellum--the Druidic god of the harvest, Samhain. Olivia recalled that Samhain had also been deemed the Lord of the Dead, and she shivered.

It was an extraordinary costume, and she had to admit it suited this exotic party Lord Quinn had chosen to host, and set the mood with its paganistic styling. She would make a point of speaking with him, of course. She must be polite. Even if the very idea of speaking to a partially nude man made her head spin, albeit not wholly unpleasantly.

She found a new glass of wine, and turned from the crowd for a half dozen quick sips.

When the music began again, louder now, she didn't give a thought to restraining herself. Why should she be alone in that? She

16

swayed to the tune, not caring if anyone should see. She was rewarded when a cavalier asked if she would join him for the dance.

"Why, 'ow lovely," she agreed at once. She set aside the near-empty wineglass and took his offered hand, swaying onto the floor at his side.

"You're new, aren't you?"

"New?"

"Among Quinn's circle," he explained. "Even though I can't see your face, I know I would have remembered you had we met before," he said, his eyes flicking down to the rounded tops of her breasts and tightly-covered waist.

She refused to take affront; she was, after all, the architect of her own appearance tonight. "Well, I know you, sir. You are Lord Tattingor." It had taken her but a moment to see beneath his simple mask. For some business purpose or other, he'd called on Stratton at their home a time or two.

"By Jove! You do know me. But, you. You are French?"

"Per'aps," she said airily.

The question in his eyes assured her, at the dance's end, that he hadn't perceived who she might be. She left his side with a laugh that refused him the right to stand and chat with her, floating about until another man claimed her for the next dance.

Perhaps it was her free laughter, or perhaps it was her bright accented chatter, or maybe even the challenge of trying to find out who she might be, but for whatever reason, she was asked to dance every dance. Between sets she had a throng of gentlemen about her, until she would laughingly bestow her hand upon the arm of the gentleman who she'd decided was to be her next partner. He would quiz her, or tease her, or whisper he had to know her name, but the only answer she would give was, "Lady Cat is name enough for me tonight."

"But how shall I ever see you again if I don't know your name?" a friar asked her.

"Per'aps you never shall." Her mirth was so contagious, he was forced to laugh with her.

Finally she sat down, denying all offers, truly a bit unsteady on her feet. It was the wine, of course, not to mention the flattery and attention she'd been receiving. It was heady stuff for one who had been so cut off from society, this mischievous play, this hedonistic night of freedoms.

As she rested, her eyes darted about the room so she'd not miss anything. Feeling as greedy as a child in a sweetshop, she became aware of a stir at her side. She turned her head slightly to the right, then more fully, as she saw that the circle of gentlemen around her had parted. Someone was stepping up to her, and was being allowed through the crush in a manner that bespoke...something. Power. Energy. Or perhaps it was the man's costume: he was dressed as Louis XIV, an odd choice in this time of war with the French. But then her eyes rose beyond his golden shoes, his white stockings, the clothing made in the style of another century, his garb as golden as the shoes. There were fine falls of lace peeping from either sleeve and at his throat, and he wore a tall curly white wig. As she met his eyes, she saw he wore no mask.

His eyes were dark, clear, and unblinking. They made his face commanding, which when added to the slight smile of greeting on his lips, gave him a strangely authoritative presence that could well explain why the other men had fallen away to let him pass. Despite the old-fashioned wig, he was handsome, and not just because one imagined a "king" ought always be handsome. She didn't know him at all, but that was not surprising, not after being hidden away for so long.

He made a motion, regal, in keeping with his outfit, to one of the men standing nearby, saying not a word. Nonetheless the man, Mr. Nantes, leaned forward to make an introduction.

"I...er...good sir, please meet Lady Cat," he managed. Olivia glanced at the kingly man briefly, then around at the others, becoming convinced by the expressions on their half-hidden faces that no one else knew, any more than she did, who this gentleman was.

The man took the "introduction" at its face value, reaching for the hand she belatedly offered and bowing over it. As she pulled her hand back into her lap, she queried, "You wear no mask, sir?"

"I have no need. I am unknown here."

"But you are English," she said, not entirely certain; there was a hint of an accent in his otherwise perfect English, wasn't there?

"I am." He gave another half-bow to acknowledge the point. "But I have not resided in England since I was a child."

So the accent was there indeed, if but a whisper. It wasn't French. What was it?

"Where 'ave you come to us from?"

He gave a small shrug of arms and shoulders definitely not learned in English ballrooms, but did not otherwise answer.

"May I 'ave your name?" she asked.

"May I have yours?"

So she was back to party games. Olivia was happy enough to play.

"No, you may not," she answered clearly, and though he might have to guess if she smiled, she allowed him to hear it in her voice.

"No?" he echoed, but then he was smiling, too. "You enjoy the true spirit of the masquerade, *mademoiselle*?"

Her married status meant he ought to have called her "*madame*," but she liked that he had not--no doubt because she wore no ring.

"I do."

He looked at her steadily, still smiling a little. She got the impression he was unsure of her, perhaps even a trifle annoyed. He surprised her, then, when he asked her to dance.

Still, she didn't hesitate. "*Oui*," she said, standing and putting out her hand as he offered her his arm.

He led her past the crowd of people feasting, talking, laughing, to a small area some intrepid dancers had carved out for themselves as a dance floor. She heard the strains of a waltz. Having learned the dance from her sister, Olivia was delighted to get to perform the daring gambol at a real party. *And no less than with a handsome, mysterious stranger.* This was why she'd come tonight, to do what she'd too seldom--or never--done before.

She'd had a few dances as a debutante, but too few. She and Stratton had danced but twice together. At two-and-seventy years old, the closest her groom had come to being of a dancing mind had been the handful of extremely awkward bedroom antics Olivia had endured with him. But at least because of Stratton she now knew men, too, had nipples...as clearly did their host.

Hoping her partner didn't feel her shudder at such thoughts, Olivia pushed her ponderings aside, and let the maskless Louis take her in his arms. She did not gasp when his fingers curled around her waist to touch the small of her back. However, she was a bit shocked by the movement of the dance, for they swayed so close to one another. It was one thing to be face-to-face with one's sister, but quite another to be held by a man almost as though in an embrace. No wonder many people still found the dance to be shocking. This Louis had them circling, swirling, making sure the wine she'd drunk rushed to her head. He danced well, the nature of his movements revealing this was not the first time he'd danced the waltz. She allowed herself to be swept along by him, her face becoming flushed with pleasure underneath her mask.

Oh, dancing was such a delight! And her partner chatted easily. His hand stayed in place on her waist, thank goodness. What if it had slipped down onto her bottom, like was happening with a couple dancing nearby? She'd simply back out of his arms and dash away, she decided, not caring if she offended her partner or her host.

Fortunately, the Louis who held her knew how to act the gentleman. *A fair dancer and well-behaved?* She began to chat more easily as she chose to trust him for the length of the dance.

Moving with this man was a far cry from dancing with Phoebe. Or even walking with Stratton at her side. Olivia became acutely aware of the smoothness of a young hand touching hers, of the lack of a stoop or a limp, of a mouth that retained all its teeth. The wine in her head no longer made her feel dizzy, but buoyed. She found she really could no longer be sure she'd heard any accent in the man's voice. If his claim of spending his childhood away from England was true, surely he'd been raised by English nannies? Anyway, English had surely been his first language. Not that it mattered; what mattered was that she'd come out tonight in order to be seen, and this graceful man made her feel he was seeing a bit of her self, despite her mask, and not finding her wanting.

After the dance, he gave her a gallant leg worthy of Louis XIV himself, and led her to the side of the dancing area. His expression was now the reverse of what it had been earlier--now his mouth was sober but his eyes were glittering. It was as though something had occurred, something...well, the only word she could think of to explain her impressions was "exciting"...and that he was making a studied effort not to acknowledge it, either by word or expression. Only his eyes, alight in his face, could not hide the knowledge, speaking eyes that seemed to be saying something in a language she could not quite understand. For a moment, she felt the old, habitual reserve slipping over her again, but she firmly thrust it aside. She opened her mouth to speak, not knowing what she meant to say...anything--but he spoke first.

"I must see to something, dear lady, and therefore must leave your side for now. But please tell me you will still be here for the entertainments that I hear will come after *midnight*?"

Why had he put that little bit of emphasis on midnight? Did he wish to see her without a mask before he committed more time or attention to her? For that matter, was he a bit too eager to abandon her? The huffy feeling that stole over her stung more than a little...but only lasted a moment as she admitted to herself, *As you've done to others all evening.*

Pushing notions of injury aside, and even though she'd had no intention of staying, she nodded. "I zink I might," she said, amazed at the breathlessness of her own voice. It had been caused by the dancing, of course.

He bowed again, taking up her hand just long enough to give her a long look--which, again, gave her pause. She turned away at once, hoping the gesture left him with the impression she was not overly concerned about a meeting that might happen later.

Quickly surrounded by a circle of admiring gentlemen, Olivia gratefully allowed one of them to take her into a country dance. Once out of King Louis's arms, she wasn't quite sure what to make of the stranger.

She relegated the experience to the back of her mind, knowing there was time enough to think again about the mysterious Louis XIV once midnight crept nearer.

# Chapter 2

Ian Drake, the new Viscount Ewald, leaned against a column in his king's garb, as open to public view as a man could be in such a crowded room. His arms were crossed behind his back, against the column, giving him the look of any other indolent young buck in the room, if one looked beyond the too-warm white wig he wore.

He'd arrived expecting to meet someone tonight. The only problem came from the fact he didn't know who that someone was to be. *Hadn't known,* he tested the thought; had he found the French informer? *Perhaps, perhaps.*

Ian tried to look around with eyes that weren't too greedy. Yes, he was here to enact one last duty, but far more importantly, at least to him, was the fact he'd come home. *I am surrounded by Englishmen. These are my people.* By the length of but one day, he'd come to the land he'd been increasingly longing for from afar. He'd not been within her borders for nearly twenty years, not since he was seven.

He'd been to a hundred parties not too dissimilar to this, amid the British who, like he and his small family, had resided away from their land of birth. He believed he knew how to behave--but all the same, he watched these mostly untraveled compatriots with eager, questing eyes. *Who are you? Among you, who am I?*

One thing he knew he was: yet a mourner. It was not four months since Mama and Papa had died, carried away by typhus. They'd survived insurrections, and rioting, and once the attack of a knife-wielding servant who'd been placed in their household to spy upon them. Afterward Ian had not even hated the man, whom Papa had clubbed into insensibility with a fireplace poker before turning him over to authorities--for his parents and he had all been spies themselves, and knew the risks of traveling and scheming abroad for King and Country. His brother, Arthur, had been the most disconcerted, because his eyes were already turning to the sea, his part in any espionage being only because he belonged with his family. Still, the unexpected was all a part of how life unfolded in unsettled places where England required prying eyes. They'd lived in three meager rooms without doors between the four of them, and they'd lived in a grand chalet with a third floor they'd never figured a way to fill or use. They'd seen filth and squalor, and they'd walked on the finest carpets on majestic marble floors. They'd seemed somehow blessed to reside above the touch of the sickness and poverty ever to be found. Yet in the end, with Arthur long since off to his naval career, it had been but a common disease that had taken Papa and a day later, Mama.

Fourteen sluggish weeks after, Papa's solictors' letter had reached Ian in Bombay--informing him of something he'd known but little considered: Ian was now the second Viscount Ewald. He was bid to come "home" and assume his duties.

An assumption he could have blithely ignored...except he'd been increasingly thinking about the green island of his birth. He remembered rain, and horses snorting in cool morning air, and pleasant summers that did not bake the sense right out of your head. Even before his parents had passed, hadn't he been wondering why the charms of Athens, St. Petersburg, or Madrid had started to pale? Hadn't he begun to ask himself what was home? Hadn't he begun to envy Arthur his place upon a ship, his clear duty? Had his

24

employment begun to pall because he was never settled anywhere for long? What was his future to be, and where?

And now he was the viscount... Which, among other things, meant there was the responsibility to marry. Only of late, now there was also a *desire* to do so. He would build a new family--but first he must come back his homeland, where he would find his helpmeet.

So, he'd answered the solicitors's beckoning, and on the long sea journey had truly begun to not only accept but crave the new life promised him by his old country.

However, the previously unknown commander who'd met him on the London dock as he'd come down *The Rajah's* gangplank had asked one more task of him. "Here in England, you're unknown, and that's exactly what we require," Sir Terrence had told him, stroking his mustache to either side with a finger. "Your monarch asks just one more task of you, that you await our informer's approach, and you keep this person safe and hidden until secret transport can be arranged."

"'This person'?" Ian had echoed.

"*Secret*," Sir Terrence had repeated.

Ian had given it only a minute's consideration, then nodded his acceptance, taking a written invitation and a fat bag pressed into his hands, and assented to this one last, minor duty.

So for this night he'd dressed out of the bag as a French king--a heavy hint for the unknown informer--and had gone completely unmasked. He had but to wait for the informer to find him at the masquerade.

Or had she already? The lady in the cat costume--she'd had a French accent.

Although, had it been imperfect? Was she faking the accent? Or was she a Frenchwoman trying to echo English tones? If she was trying to hide from French retribution, it would behoove her to try to sound less French...

25

Certainly, she had gone to some effort to hide her person, if not her form. She'd made her features unknowable, and yet the revealing cut of her gown was arguably more French than English. He'd thought before that the informer could be either a man or a woman, and now he began to remeasure the chance it was the latter. After all, the best place to hide was in a crowd. Especially a crowd where everyone was pretending to be something other than they truly were.

And Lord Quinn's crowd was an unusual one, make no mistake about that.

Ian turned casually toward a group of smiling revelers, looking into their masked faces, reading the things they said with how they moved, how they placed their bodies. He nodded confirmation at his own thought that he might have found the person he sought.

Yet, years of training told him not to be convinced, not quite yet, that the Lady Cat was his mark.

***

Across the room a woman dressed like a harvest gleaner--complete with an apron over her unrealistically pristine homespun cloth gown, a kerchief tied about her head, no mask, and a basket of *papier mâché* fall fruits--surveyed the room in her turn. The woman made note of every person she could not identify at once and went through the crowd, meeting each until she was sure of their identity. Only a handful of masks proved any challenge.

She knew that an informant, a traitor, had escaped France. She knew this because of the last missive that had been carried to her back door, late at night when all the servants were asleep except for her apprehensive maid Sophie, who brought her any notes and never dared to breathe a word to anyone about them, not with her parents still held in France.

It was the "gleaner's" newest charge to help learn the location of the escaped informant in England, no doubt meant to make his way to Scotland, the path of other escapees before him. It was her duty to be observant, to provide any information or action needed to stop his flight from justice. Traitors against France must be dealt with, and harshly.

After circling the room, she was satisfied there were only two things she did not know: who was the man dressed as Louis XIV? And who was the woman in the cat costume?

Their unexplained appearances here, in the wake of the knowledge she had received just last night, was suspect. Neither of them was the informant--he wouldn't dare appear at a *haute ton* affair such as this, surely?

But strangers knew about strange things. It behooved her to make the acquaintance of King and Cat.

***

Not too far outside London, a man swore silently in virulent French. The carriage door was opened for him, but he did not need to climb down from the coach onto the dark road to know a wheel had broken. The terrible crunch and sudden list to the right had told him that.

"How far to walk to the Lord Quinn's?" He spoke slowly, carefully, trying to sound English. He didn't think he'd succeeded.

The driver scratched his head and considered. "It'd take ya' the better part of an hour, I s'pose."

The man, Georges Douzain, swore in his head, and gestured at the broken wheel. "Repair it! Quickly!"

The driver tugged at a forelock of dark hair in acknowledgement of the command, and motioned toward the inn only a hundred yards or so up the road. "There's wine or ale to be had, no doubt," he told his only passenger. "Pr'aps a horse to be hired?"

Douzain, despite fear and vexation growing by the moment, shook his head. He was safer hidden inside an inn, then back in the coach. "I will wait for you. But you must 'urry." He reached into the carriage to pull out a stuffed bag, all he had brought with him in

27

this world, and began to walk the road. He kept his hat down and his collar up, even long after he had begun to warm by the inn's fire, wishing he could afford a private room. The inn boasted a long clock, and Douzain swore quietly again to see it was nearing eleven; midnight approached far too fast.

# Chapter 3

Olivia watched Lord Quinn turn over a tarot card where he sat before a small table, and saw the light from a simple brace of candles dance in his eyes. He was very good at setting a mood. Olivia almost laughed at the absurd notion that watching for glimpses of his nipple was somehow less intimate than taking in one of his bare feet not covered by the table's linen, or the sheerness of sleeves that scarcely covered his muscled arms. Part of her wanted to look away from his shocking ensemble--but part dared her to keep accepting his unspoken dare. Those others who stood about his barely lit table also seemed compelled to lean forward, to take in his appearance as well as try to spot what fate this irregular man saw spelled out among the cards.

The young blonde lady who sat posed before him gave a nervous little smile, a reflection of the pastime's dark edge, one that Quinn's very presence only increased. The night lent itself, too, to the game, with moonlit fog arms drifting past the windows as the midnight hour approached. Perhaps Lord Quinn ought to have been dressed as a gypsy to indulge in this game of fortune-telling, but his eerie, brazen appearance and the very low light lent to the persuasion that he could indeed read one's future.

"What did that last card tell you?" the girl asked in a hushed voice, her eyes fixed to his face, which was gathered in a serious, pensive pose.

He turned over another card, and one eyebrow shot up toward the horn balanced above it, even while the corners of his mouth turned down. He looked at the fair-haired girl without lifting his chin. "Has something gone missing recently?"

Her eyes rounded, and her hand sprang to her hair. "Mama's diamond-set comb," she breathed. "I lost it. She was most vexed with me. Do you know where it is?"

He turned over another card. "The Hanged Man," he noted softly.

The girl gasped. "Am I going to die?"

Quinn lifted his head now, giving her a tolerant look. "No. The Hanged Man represents change, not death. Although death can be a change, certainly." He smiled, and the candle flickers made the smile more sinister. One corner of Olivia's mouth tilted up in appreciation; she was more than half sure he knew the effect of the room's dimness. "But, see, it is inverted. Which implies the opposite. Being stuck, without change." He turned over two more cards. "I am afraid the comb may be beyond retrieval."

"Truly lost?" the girl pouted.

"Or...stolen."

Her pout turned into a scowl. "Are you telling me Anthony took it? That he *sold* it? For his gaming debts?"

Quinn made a gesture over the cards. "I see only that what is gone is beyond recovery."

"That blackguard." The blonde's hands clenched on the table top. "It's just like Anthony."

Several of the observers whispered among themselves, confirming Anthony was the girl's brother, while they enjoyed the drama of the moment.

"Then tell me this," the girl said, words clipped. "How soon will I box my brother's ears?"

Lord Quinn's head tilted a little to the right, and a slight, perhaps not quite sincere smile formed as he spread several more cards. But the young lady seemed not to notice he was indulging her temper. He considered the cards for a long moment, then cried out, "Beware!" in a storyteller's voice.

Even though she was certain he was merely play-acting, the tenor of Quinn's voice sent shivers down Olivia's spine. A murmur rippled through the gathered witnesses, proving it had the same effect on them. "You must be careful of a marriage," he intoned, "a marriage just ahead."

The girl bit her lip, distress replacing vexation. Another murmur rose and fell, for it was well known the young lady's wedding was only a fortnight away.

"Be careful," Lord Quinn repeated eerily, giving new life to the rumors that the man was "different," even "bizarre." Card readings were severely frowned upon by the Church; she'd been in his company for only a handful of minutes, but it was easy to believe he flouted their censure, or indeed anyone's.

He smiled then at the girl, a slow roll of his lips. "Be careful...be very careful," he drew out the words, then rushed ahead, "not to sleep late on November fourteenth, or you'll miss your own wedding."

The crowd gave a relieved laugh, and the bride sat back with an audible sigh of reprieve. She rose then, shaking her head, her relief taking her laughter into a titter.

"Are there others who wish to know their future?" Lord Quinn asked the crowd as he shuffled the cards between his two hands. There was a sudden silence, and furtive glances, but no one spoke up. It seemed the young bride had not been the first customer to be discomfited by the night's spell and Lord Quinn's uncanny execution of his little game.

Olivia stepped forward. She was not disconcerted, not really. She welcomed the tingle of the forbidden. "I would like to know my fortune, *Monsieur* my lord."

He smiled, and again the two flickering candles only served to make his expression unsettling. So she sat with a flourish. How could she call herself daring, come the morning, if she couldn't face a mere card-reading?

***

Ian turned from the group with which he had been standing, his sharp ears hearing the French accent that drifted through a doorway leading to a mostly darkened room. He made his excuses and passed through the doorway, seeing a brace of candles barely managed to highlight an attentive group--including the woman with the maybe-French accent. He crossed to see what had attracted the Lady Cat to this smaller gathering.

The night's host, Lord Quinn, was shuffling a deck of cards, but his eyes were only for the masked cat seated on the opposite side of the table from him. It was clear Quinn tried to see beyond the cat's face to the hidden woman. Ian saw the man give up the direct attempt, unable to know her that way. He crossed his arms and settled in to see if Quinn could bring anything forth from the lady.

Quinn laid out three cards, hmmming. His eyes flicked up once, settling on the lady's bosom, as though it might be familiar to him where nothing else had been so far. Then he looked back to the cards and pronounced, "It is my great fortune to inform you the cards say your coming New Year will be a prosperous one."

One of Ian's hands rose to cup his chin. If the Lady Cat was the informer, why put herself forward this way? Again, was she hiding by not hiding?

The crowd grumbled, dissatisfied with Quinn's conclusion. Dire or wayward predictions were ever so much more fun.

"Is zere no more?" the Cat asked, sounding amused. Ian noted the bit of ankle that showed under her skirts where she sat, and took a moment to admire the bit of stockinged leg revealed.

"There is more," Lord Quinn said, his eyes rising to hers again. One could not tell in this light, but earlier Ian had noted the man had deep blue eyes, which now danced even in the dimness. "They also reveal that you are to meet a man. A dark-haired man. He will become your lover."

The crowd reacted with appreciation--this was more in the way of what they wished to hear.

The lady's eyes moved to Lord Quinn's own hair, which was dark, only a few strands of scattered gray caught by the candles's light. There was something in the set of her shoulders that hinted at a reprimand forming--but then she surprised Ian by giving a full-throated laugh.

Lord Quinn startled, too, at the gaiety of her laughter. By his expression, Ian judged the man had not anticipated such a response from the unknown lady either. But then the crowd was laughing, too, and Quinn along with them. He shook a finger at the woman. "Lady, you intrigue me. Before the night is out I must know either your face or your name." There was something more in the man's look, though, and Ian frowned to think Lord Quinn's unspoken thought might be he desired more than just the woman's name.

Ian's hand came away from his chin slowly, his arms uncrossing, and he suddenly believed this woman was the informant. He believed it because she was clever, as an informant would need to be. Too, having spent an hour now at Quinn's masquerade, Ian had not been slow to see the sensual tenor of the gathering. Despite the come-hither cut of her bodice, he was becoming increasingly convinced the Cat did not belong among this crowd. She had flirted lightly with him when they'd danced--but she'd turned her gaze away from the groping couple dancing nearby. She'd floated among the participants but, until the tarot, had not joined them in their peculiar games. She was, for this throng, behaving with circumspection.

So then, why hadn't she approached him and let him know for a certainty she was the informant? It was true they'd been meant to make contact at midnight, but why had she chosen to be so visible earlier than the appointed hour? Or had he made her uncertain, since he'd approached her too soon? He'd been distracted, taking in these Englishmen he meant to rejoin; he ought to have waited, been more precise.

Well, he would know better at midnight, surely, if she came then to his side? He could wait another half hour.

Then again, why wait, when a few words could clear up the question? If she was not the right contact, he must be free when midnight did roll around.

As the crowd commented to one another, smiling and jostling, Lord Quinn set aside the deck of cards with a firm hand, indicating he was done with this game for the night. He made to rise, but before he could lean forward to offer the unknown lady his arm, Ian had stepped up to do the same.

"Another dance, my lady?" he asked.

Lady Cat looked up, clearly not having known he was there. She seemed to hesitate a moment, but then she inclined her head.

"My pleasure," she murmured as she stood and took his arm.

"I say!" someone called as Ian made to pull her from the room and toward the dance floor. "Is this the bloke then? The 'dark-haired lover'?"

"Nah, he's not dark-haired," called another.

The gathering gave a group sound of disappointment, but then Ian reached up and pulled the white wig off to reveal his own short, curly dark hair beneath. Truth to tell, he was grateful for the excuse to remove the hot, heavy thing, which he tossed aside now. The crowd gave a cry of appreciation, as he turned to see the Cat's surprised eyes looking at him out of her mask.

Did he now look more as he'd been described to her? As soon as he had her away and on the dance floor, he'd know if she were the one.

\*\*\*

Alexander, Lord Hargood, turned at the tug on his sailor costume's sleeve, disappointed that among this licentious crowd it was but his oldest sister, Phoebe, trying to snare his attention. She was dressed in some elaborate ensemble he supposed was meant to represent a sheik's lady, as it was comprised of multiple layers of shimmering cloth bedecked with multiple faux jewels, and a diaphanous veil "covered" (if that was the right word for something that was all but completely sheer) all of her face but her eyes. She said rather quietly near his ear, "Do you see that woman there?"

He looked in the direction her bejeweled hand indicated, and perceived his sister meant the woman in the cat ensemble. The woman was just coming from a darkened room, on the arm of the unknown fellow all made up like a French king, except now his wig was gone. Alex turned his attention away from the dark-haired man, back to the costumed cat, and replied in an appreciative tone, "Indeed. She's quite the little baggage, isn't she?"

He received a dark look for his efforts. "Ninny!" jeered Phoebe, her face-veil fluttering. "Don't you know who that is?"

"Wish I did," was his reply, his chin going up in defiance of his oldest sister's proclamation. He didn't tell her that the lady had already caught his eye. He had just recently given up his mistress and was looking for some other likely creature to replace her. Tired of opera dancers, he'd agreed to escort Phoebe tonight because he'd hoped to see what his own circle had to offer in that regard. And there had been this lovely little minx, all disguised, showing a bit of ankle, playing at flirting, with charms evident for any who cared to admire them.

"Well?" prompted Phoebe with a second irritated tug at his sleeve. "Do you know who that is?"

"No thought at all."

Phoebe let out an exasperated sigh, leaning even more closely to him to whisper in the quietest voice, "'Tis Olivia."

His head whipped up at that, his eyes changing at once from appreciation, to doubt, to denial. Could this hoyden be their middle sibling? "Olivia!" he cried in a hoarse whisper. "Olivia's in mourning. Never goes anywhere. And she'd never show up in a rig like...like that!"

"I tell you it's her. Only listen when she laughs."

Alexander turned and squinted at the masked woman, waiting for one of the trills of laughter she'd been emitting all evening, one of which came a minute later. His face registered astonishment, his ears having recognized where his eyes had been unable to do so. "Great heavens," he said under his breath. "I believe you're right." He started forward, his intention to haul his sister away evident in every line of his body.

Once again his arm was caught, but this time firmly held. "Alexander," scolded Phoebe. "You can't do that. Then everyone here will know exactly who she is."

His cravat felt uncomfortably tight as he glanced away from Olivia's unseemly expanse of bosom to Phoebe's forbidding look. "You can't expect me to do nothing," he sputtered.

"I can, and I do. I suspect Olivia knows what she's doing."

"I'm not so sure. And why did you call my attention to this fact if you don't expect me to correct the situation?"

"Because you were making calf's eyes at her."

"I most certainly was not!"

"You were. But do not fret over it. Every man here is doing the same, and how can you be blamed, for I must admit this...this display is very unlike her." She lifted her chin, a sign of support. "But I say 'brava.' She's desperately needed to enter society again. I could never fathom why she hid away in that house for so long. Surely a year would have been sufficient? I took off my black for her Stratton after three months. I mean, I scarcely knew him." She shuddered; she'd never envied Olivia's marriage, having her own much happier one. "Olivia's been in black so long, poor dear. But she clearly has some plan, being here tonight, and I say leave her to it. I want your agreement on this, Alex."

"What, that I'll let my sister make a cake of herself?"

"Lower your voice, please." There were several persons who had turned their way, noting the rise in Alexander's tone--including a woman dressed as a peasant gleaner who stared through the simple stretch of black fabric that served as her mask, enough of a stare to cause Phoebe to half turn away. "Just pretend you still don't know who she is, that's all. And let her go about her business."

"Business?" Alexander scoffed, crossing his arms over his chest and scowling darkly.

"Your promise, Alex, or else I'll not leave your side all night."

That was a dire threat, for there was nothing so damping to one's love life as a sister on one's sleeve. His conscience and his inclination warred for a moment in the stubborn set of his face, until finally he burst out, "All right then! You have my promise. But only for tonight. If I ever see Olivia doing the like again, well then, I'll not stand by, I won't."

"'Tis a bargain," Phoebe agreed, keeping her end of the agreement by moving away at once.

She moved into the crowd, but not so far back that she was unable to observe, unnoticed, as Olivia went into the arms of the handsome monarch for a second dance.

Phoebe bit her lip, her eyes observant; she could not say just how far Olivia would dare go. She loved her younger sister...but she knew she'd neglected her sibling, and knew her too little. Phoebe had married first, had five children, a husband, and a household to manage, and had little time for the sister more cruelly affected by their parents' deaths.

She'd pretended to Alexander that she understood Olivia's choice to come to this startling masquerade--she'd come herself in order to boast of being modern and broadminded--but, truth was, she was not at all sure she knew what Olivia hoped to achieve on this quite possibly wicked night.

# Chapter 4

It was not the waltz this time. It was a country dance Ian shared with the Lady Cat.

He could see too little of her face. The tip of her chin might be that of a hundred ladies. Her green eyes were distinctive, although the mask might be interfering with knowing their true hue. He thought her hair must be a rich blonde, but the wisp that had escaped her hood was but a few hairs, making it difficult in candlelight to be sure. It was frustrating, as though he might know her if only he could see behind the mask, but of course that was false. Everyone here tonight was unknown to him. A series of French ladies he had known over the years crossed his mind, all to be dismissed.

"Where did you live in France?" he asked as they moved together.

"Here. Zere," she said as the dance moved her away from his side.

He was a little surprised by her caution--surely it would be simple to answer "Paris," or half a dozen cities large enough for her to claim, whether true or not. But of course this was not the most auspicious time to be a Frenchman in England, even though there had been a large host of émigrés escaping the Corsican's tyranny. She was being cautious, making enquiries more difficult; that was commendable, in his experience.

"My dear," he said when they came back together in the pattern of the dance, "it is close in here. Shall we retire to the garden for a few moments?"

If he had doubted her, he was reassured by her agreement to this plan. "Oh, yes, fresh air, *s'il vous plaît*," she breathed.

She picked up a glass of wine as they left the dance and trailed across the crowded room toward the garden doors. He echoed her action, choosing a glass of his own before taking her hand on his arm and leading her out into the evening. If this loose-moraled crowd minded, the two of them would appear a young, frivolous couple taking some air and a chance for unobserved flirtation.

***

Lord Quinn watched the couple depart through the doors into his garden, and caught the arm of the woman who was passing by, his hostess. She was dressed as a gleaner. He whispered in her ear, quickly, shortly, received a nod in return, and released her arm. She wordlessly slipped away, and Quinn turned back to his guests with a show of deportment and only a mildly preoccupied manner.

***

"Oh, look," Olivia said as they stepped into the garden. "Lord Quinn 'as 'ad the garden decorated. It gives the shivers, no?"

Ian glanced around, seeing the various sheets hung from trees, serving as breeze-moved ghosts, revealed by the half-light that spilled from the house. There were oversized turnips carved with faces on them, an old obscure Scottish practice, their carved white faces made to glow by a candle set within. The scene concocted by their host was accented by the increasing fog, and by the feeble moonlight. There was a definite chill in the air, but after the closeness of the party, it was not unwelcome and perhaps added a bit to the tendency--not wholly unpleasant--to want to shiver indeed.

"Our host seeks to entertain us," he said in response as he glanced about, taking note of several other pairs of strollers. "Come," he said,

40

taking her arm, "let us venture forth and see if there are more surprises our host has arranged for us."

There were no fairy lamps hung about, as one might usually find in a garden open to partygoers, no doubt to be in keeping with the theme of the revelry, spooky and mysterious.

Ian gave the Lady Cat a sideways glance. Her ready agreement to leave the masquerade had made him think she was prepared to flee with him--but now she seemed genuinely appreciative of the garden decorations, like a mere partygoer.

It was time to be clear with one another.

Ahead he saw the glimmer of a building's outline. He hadn't known it was there, for his brief scouting run earlier today had not included trespassing on Lord Quinn's property. He had merely ascertained there was an apparent path through the garden to the alley behind, where he had ordered a carriage to await his arrival, with the lateness of the rendezvous hour unknown.

Now he held the hand of the costumed lady, trying to saunter so as not to appear peculiarly at haste. Closer, he saw through the fog that the small building had no door, and he led her within. A perfect place to stop and ascertain that they'd not been followed before they went on, making good on their escape.

*** 

Olivia pulled her hand free as soon as she crossed the little building's threshold. It was a simple structure, perhaps once a two-horse stable, and had the smell of dirt and rusting metal that showed it had been converted over to tool storage. There was a glassless window, which framed the fog-shrouded moon. It was very dark within.

*Why did he bring me here?* she asked herself...but something deep inside her knew the most logical explanation.

He turned to her, taking her glass, and placing both hers and his on the window sill. "Let us speak frankly. You seek escape?" he said.

Olivia stared. How had he been able to see that she was trying so very hard not to be herself tonight? Was she so transparent as all that?

He'd asked her to be frank, and she chose to comply. Still, it was so dark that he might not be able to tell from how she held herself that there were limits, so she made her accented voice crisp. "Yes. But I am not, how you say? Not a tart."

He'd been peering out the window frame, but now he turned. It was hard to say, since she could only pick out a single moon-silvered line to give her the notion of his profile, but she thought he moved as though startled. "Nor did I call you one."

She swallowed. "I zought you brought me," she glanced around, unenchanted, "'ere to 'ave a...a tryst?"

And what if he had? Had she hoped for it? A bit of inappropriateness? Or...more? She'd been married. She knew what sexual congress was. So long as no child came of the act, in what way could it harm her? She knew women sometimes had lovers. Why not her? Why not just once? To see if it could be something ...more. If she retained her mask, and let him use her body...well, who would be using whom? Surely the night was yet too young, too precious a treat to be let go of already? Such an adventure she was having. Was it to be a much greater, much more thrilling exploration?

He stared at her, and she stared back even though all they could see was the faintest outline of one another. A stranger in the dark, talking to another stranger... She wanted to shock, and to be startled herself. She caught a scent of woodsy soap, and breathed it in deeply. Something about the intimate aroma of a man's soap made her want to abandon thought. When had she ever even had a chance to misbehave?

"A tryst? Mademoiselle, I don't know what--"

"I zink," she gave a throaty little sound that even she wasn't sure was a laugh. "I zink I just would like you to kiss me."

He straightened a little, drawing back half a step.

She gave him no more time to think, stepping against him, raising the mask and slipping it over her head. Her hair fell free as she pulled it out of the short domino, and maybe even in the deep dark he could tell her hair was light-colored.

"*Mademoiselle--*"

She put a hand on both of his shoulders, coming up on tiptoe, shocked by her own daring but caught up in it all the same. No, there would be no lovemaking, she was not such a fool. But one kiss? One kiss, and she would flee, taking her mask and her gown and herself home, to savor over and over in memory the night she'd dared to be a bit wild and free and irresponsible and careless. It didn't matter that her head was swimming; indeed, it only added to the moment, only made her more determined to give herself the shocking thrill of an unknown man's lips on her own.

He remained still for a moment, but then, slowly, he leaned down to her, the minimal light causing him to first find her cheek with his mouth. For a moment she thought that would be the extent of the moment, but she decided it would not and turned her head, causing his lips to slide across her cheek and find her mouth with his own.

For all that Olivia had been married, she'd scarce been kissed. She anticipated a dry peck--not the sliding together of warm, firm lips.

It began a fine enough thing, a salute, but then his mouth pressed hers a bit more fully. It took only a few seconds more before she knew his was not a kiss she'd known before, oh no indeed. Those given to Mama, and Papa, and even Stratton, they had been familial toasts. Expected, but a thing made from duty, not attraction. They'd been *nothing* like this man-woman exchange that deepened by the moment, a thing of awareness, and sensation, and a growing need to sink deeper yet.

Gasping, Olivia drew back, enough to look up into glittering eyes whose color she knew to be brown but were little more than shadows now. One of his hands remained yet on her waist. She shuddered, unable to keep from letting him feel the shiver, and acutely aware her universe had shifted, her knowledge of the world expanded.

"I didn't know," she whispered.

"Know?"

"That it could feel so...special," she said, knowing he would not see her profound blush, and grateful for it. "I thought it was all fairy stories."

"Yes?"

They peered through the dark at each other, but then he was drawing her in again, kissing her, except this time not so gently, not so kindly. It was, though, just as sweet, sweeter than any wine. She offered no resistance, instead leaning into him all the more. She found she'd forgotten she'd meant to share a single kiss. She'd also forgotten the elemental wonder of a touch; there was a timelessness, a lack of thought, that came with a caress. It didn't matter that they didn't know each other, it only mattered that for a moment they were connected in excitement and want and a magic she hadn't known existed.

Finally he raised his mouth, and he gave a quiet laugh. The sound, so warm and male and charming, made her tremble again in his arms.

"Thank you, *mademoiselle*," he said. The angle of his head kept adjusting just a tiny bit, and she thought he must be doing as she did, trying to somehow part the darkness the better to see. She smiled at his tone, one hand touching the lay of his coat front in a familiar way that managed to not feel awkward. The gesture was an unspoken word of thanks in return.

The mood changed. She was quite sure it was because of their closeness, their mingled breathing. She felt his hand slide along her arm, catching up her hand and holding it between them. She was glad there was no ring there for him to feel.

"Are you ready?" he asked.

She drew in a breath. "Ready? For...more dalliance?"

He laughed softly. "That was not what I meant, but..." He let his voice trail away, and one arm slipped around her lower back, pulling her even closer.

And she let him. She not only let him, but some part of her wondered if, despite her best intentions, she'd stop him from doing anything he desired at all?

*** 

How odd, Ian thought, to find that this nameless woman had climbed into his arms. Worse, she'd touched something in his chest; he felt his heart as its steady thumping began to accelerate just because she stood pressed against him.

Of course, she could be any sort of scoundrel. An actress. A manipulator, trying to attach herself to a rescuer. In fact, she probably was all those things...but, by God, she was also difficult to resist when she went up on tiptoe again and lifted her mouth toward his once more.

How peculiar that he could have only given a few details about her appearance, but her demeanor somehow told him she'd been wounded. Was it in the cautious touch of her hand on his chest? The way she waited for him to kiss the lips that were but a breath away from his? The way she trembled?

*Devil take me,* Ian uttered to himself just before he answered her irresistible summons and kissed her again, now allowing added flickers of ardor to communicate from his mouth to hers. She didn't shy away, instead clinging to him, seemingly thirsty for his touch.

It was as if they spoke without words, conversed and understood and smiled at each other even though their mouths were upon each other's, their hands unexpectedly tangled in each other's hair. He felt the pins that held her chignon in place fall away, even as thought had fallen away. Now it was only her and him. There was only here and now, and their two selves, and a growing, gnawing need stretching between them.

He knew the moment was altering, tumbling out of his control. He was not a man of impulse, yet he was one who had a regard for poetry, a thing of which this embrace, this woman's lips on his was made. A cadence, a rightness, almost an inevitability stirred in him, and it was only with a great effort that he made an attempt to pull away.

"I think--" he said against her lips, but she silenced him with her mouth recapturing his.

The time of protest passed. He felt her revel in his kiss, in the arms that tightened around her, and the hands that rumpled her dress and sought knowledge of her contours. The tight bodice was both revealing and frustrating, leaving little room for seeking fingers.

He didn't know how it had come to this; he had never done anything like this before, for it was clear where the moment was leading. The blood thundering through his body, and her touches in return, told him he was not mistaken. He had known women before, of course, but not even in some of the exotic locales in which he had grown as a man and as a spy had he found himself in such a position. Once or twice he'd wondered if he might have to make his way into a woman's bed to obtain the information he wanted, but other factors had always intervened. Now there was no need for such an experience; this woman had nothing he needed. She was the one who had need, to be established under a new identity, hidden from the reach of French revenge. It made no sense. He could not fathom why she was so receptive to him, a stranger, but then her tongue ventured into his mouth to touch his own, and he forgot to wonder at anything but sensation.

Suddenly, a flurry of sound came from the house, fanfares and cheers. To Ian's ears came the cries of, "Remove your masks! Remove your masks!"

He and the unnamed lady went still.

"It must be midnight," she murmured against his lips.

A long beat went by, and then she pushed against his chest, getting her feet firmly under her. He slowly let her go, even though it was the last thing his arms wanted to do.

She bent, presumably to retrieve her hair hood and mask.

"My carriage is not far--" he began to offer.

"Oh, no, you don't need to do that. I'll make my own way home."

"Home?" he echoed, confused.

She stepped up to him, one hand cupping his cheek, that she might know where to raise her lips for a quick peck on his cheek, now not lover-like but tender and sincere. "Thank you," she whispered. She stepped back toward the doorless opening, turning and crossing over the threshold of the building. She hesitated there a moment, her outline picked out in the doorway, and whispered sincerely, again, "Thank you so much." Then she stepped away.

"But--!" he cried, coming to the doorway, a hand on either side of the opening. Where was she going? Had he misunderstood his instructions somehow?

"Good night. God bless," she called softly as she slipped out of sight behind shrubbery and fog, but not before he saw the lightness of her hair disappear, presumably beneath the cat-mask's attendant hood.

"But how shall I find you?" he cried, starting forward, only to check his progress as a thought occurred to him. Did she think they'd been seen? Was she laying some kind of false trail, unbeknownst to or understood by him? But...?

Had he not been concentrating so on the lady's retreat, he might have noted a faint stirring in the slender trees off to the left. A single

47

shadow separated itself from the leaves and branches, the long gown of the dark costume evident in the night for a moment in silhouette, to slip toward the house, to complete her assigned duty by a murmur in Lord Quinn's ear.

Instead Ian heard only the Lady Cat's gentle disembodied voice as it floated back to him, "You're not meant to find me, sir."

He bit his lower lip; he could have stopped her but had not. It would have been simple to dash forward and hold her back, but he hadn't so much as moved toward her because he'd suddenly had a sinking feeling that he'd attached himself to the wrong person.

He groaned aloud when it struck him, standing there staring into the fickle fog: the mysterious Lady Cat had entirely lost her French accent.

# Chapter 5

Georges Douzain had been at the party for ten minutes, nine minutes longer than he had thought to. *I am sticking out like the thumb that is sore.*

And, worse, now he must step out from the shadows against the wall, forcing himself into the brighter light of the overhanging chandeliers. Only the fact he wore a domino to cover his head, and a cloth mask covering all but his mouth, gave him the courage to do so. He could not locate *le vicomte*; my lord Ewald must find him, it seemed.

Or was perhaps my lord Ewald already gone? It was a very poor thing Georges had arrived so late--that *stupide* carriage wheel!--it was now a quarter hour past midnight. Was it possible *le vicomte* had so soon tired of waiting, or had become convinced that he, Georges, was not going to show? The man was supposed to be in plain sight. If Georges's contact was here, the man had made himself too hard to find.

Georges circled the room one last time with only faintly hopeful eyes, peering at groups of people to see if he had overlooked anyone, but then his blood froze. *Sacre bleu!* He was caught! There was a woman, her mask abandoned presumably at midnight, one who he knew could betray him, who could send her hired thugs to hit him over the head and drag him back to his merciless fate in France. She was standing there right before him. He could not move, terror ripping through him, for he knew the "justice" that awaited him in France was no less than death as a traitor for surrendering State secrets. He must not be taken!

Her eyes turned to him, making him give a small cry deep in his throat...but then they passed on. He watched as the woman, costumed as some kind of peasant with a basket on her arm, settled her gaze on a young man dressed as a sailor. She moved toward the man, her pace smooth but her intent deliberate.

A sliver of sanity returned to Georges, and he realized his mask was still firmly in place, hiding his distinctively hooked nose, his dark hair, and that his form was still largely disguised by the bulky domino he wore. There was nothing about his person, thus cloaked, that could give him away. That is, nothing but his own nervous behavior, he thought to himself. He must leave, at once. He would have to contact this Viscount Ewald another way. It had grown far too dangerous to remain at the masquerade.

He slipped back into the shadows and out into the night, his heart pounding as he moved with sharp eyes and careful movements, working to avoid being noticed.

***

Alexander rubbed his chin, and frowned down into his wine, because he'd much rather it was brandy, and because his middle sister had disappeared. That was, perhaps, a good thing, if it meant Olivia had taken herself and her half-clothed body home; it was not so good a thing if it meant she was closeted somewhere at this assembly with some rake who would be only too willing to accept what she seemed to be offering. Alexander had grown hopeful it was the former, for he'd circulated a great deal, peering into alcoves and opening doors to closed rooms, and even going so far as to meander through the garden--where he'd seen some amorous activities that had only lent to his concern.

Phoebe was missing, too, but that concerned him less, because she'd told him she was going to make herself scarce, in order to avoid letting Olivia take a good look at her. Her flimsy face covering must be as unsuccessful as Olivia's mask--at least to her siblings--had proved to be.

For himself, perhaps Olivia had spotted Alexander, for if she remained at the masquerade, she was evading him rather handily.

"Is something the matter?" someone asked near him.

He startled and looked up, for the voice had been marked with an accent. For a fleeting moment he thought it might be Olivia, carrying on in that silly fashion she'd adopted for the night. It was not. It was the woman clothed in gleaner's dress, who had turned and stared when Phoebe had ordered him to lower his voice earlier.

"Why...er...no. How d'you do?" he mumbled, hastily transferring his glass to his left hand, for she'd extended hers toward him. He took up her hand to execute an airy kiss over it. Foreigners especially liked that kind of thing, he knew.

She gave him a small curtsy in return. He noted the way her golden-brown hair curled out from under her kerchief, and that her lips were lightly rouged, a shocking practice however in keeping with the nature of this irreverent masquerade. There was something in her posture and in her eyes, too, that suddenly made him recall why he'd come tonight. If she'd had a mask, now that midnight had come and gone she'd abandoned it, and she looked at him with a frankly warm expression.

"May I have the pleasure of making your acquaintance?" he asked, letting a little of his sudden appreciation show in return, to see how she might respond.

"I am Miss Lyons. And you are...?" She had a charming dimple in her left cheek when she smiled.

"Lord Hargood," he said on a bow. He liked that they'd had to introduce themselves, without the usual third party involved.

Flirtation was already in place, and Alexander began to hope more was to come.

"It is a pleasure to meet you," she murmured, her voice soft and low, her accent slight and very pleasant to the ear.

He smiled at her and offered her his arm, that they might stroll and talk. Yes, there was something in the way she put her hand on his arm, and in the way she looked at him, that made him feel perhaps he'd not wasted his time at this ridiculous All Hallow's affair after all. That feeling could only be enhanced when she asked, "You have come alone to this party, my lord?"

It was with some reluctance he had to admit, "Well, no. My sister's with me."

"What a kind brother you are, to escort your sister. But is your wife not present?"

"No." He smiled, growing more and more certain of the lady. "I've no wife. Just sisters," he said, the reminder causing him to glance around the room again, feeling a little guilty that he'd forgotten about Olivia for a moment.

"Ah, I hope I do not keep you from seeing to zeir needs. It grows perhaps late for some, and it could be the late hour makes for zem a great weariness? I must not keep you--"

"No, no," he assured her at once, for she had lovely light brown eyes, a reflection of her hair, eyes that spoke in a language of their own. "The one's already gone, and the other can always presume upon a friend should she care to leave. I am a free soul. And I've taken a notion to stay a while longer. Would you care for some wine, Miss Lyons?"

The lady murmured how nice that would be, her dimple showing again, and Alexander happily waved away his last thought of regret that he had come.

***

Ian re-entered Quinn's home, moving again among the crush of the party. It seemed loud and close, but he forced himself to stay still long enough to evaluate the room. He peered hard, seeking any sign that another was there, waiting for him; his true contact--if such there was.

Although, truth be told, he also looked for *her*, the lady in cat costume. He knew she'd departed, but yet he looked to see her again.

But no, she was gone. Or, no longer in costume.

He glanced into more faces, seeking light hair and light eyes, and the certain curve of a cheek. She'd been small-framed, with a delicate waist. She'd been young; her smooth skin and youthful movement had proved that.

Ian shook himself, as though the act would straighten the thoughts that tumbled in his mind. He began to grow a little angry, for doubts made him feel stupid. He'd moved past the mind-numbing and body-pleasuring interlude in the garden. Did it even matter that he find her again? Was she meant to find him once more? Or, as he began more and more to suspect, had he been mistaken altogether?

Why had he thought she could possibly be the one he had been sent to assist? Her actions hadn't been those of a woman wishing to be rescued...had they? He set his jaw, looking at the crowd again, even while his mind was lost to conflicting facts. He could explain everything about her behavior, rationally, to himself--everything except her leaving. That made no sense. Had he been so far off the mark?

If she was not the one, then who was?

He had to admit it: he'd failed. The plans had gone awry, all because he'd been mistaken in his quarry.

He didn't make his farewells to his bizarrely dressed--call it nearly undressed--host, Lord Quinn. He slipped out the front door after quietly obtaining his three-caped cloak, and walked to his carriage, not awaiting it on the front steps as was the usual fashion. His body told his mind to relax and think about it all later, but his brain settled into a darting pace that chased his thoughts about in circles.

He slumped inside his carriage, only his dark eyes revealing the whirlwind within, while his driver clucked the horses toward home. Why had the Lady Cat gone with him to the garden, if not to make an escape?

Yet that had not been her intent at all.

So then, she was a trollop, a member of the demimonde.

But...there had been no sex. No offer of such. No exchange of monies.

His talent for reading people had always stood him in good stead in the past, but now...nothing added up. It made no sense. She'd been drinking...but then again, he'd swear she'd not been so far gone that she'd not known what she was doing.

And her responses! He would swear those had not been practiced, not like the sounds or acts of any harlot he'd ever met. Either she was very new at the trade--would such a one be so giving, so apparently moved?--or else she was indeed a very fine actress.

No. It was impossible to believe. The woman had been no strumpet. The only price she'd asked of him was more kisses.

Ah, and here was a thought: indeed, she was no informant, but perhaps a widow--or a wayward wife? One who longed for affection howsoever she might come by it? Now that made some manner of sense.

Or...perhaps she longed for a child, one her husband could not give her? But she'd worn no ring. And, of course, they'd not made love. Had she quailed when the moment had been upon her? Indeed, she'd asked nothing of him but some caresses, not even giving him a face with which to be plagued in the future.

He shook himself wholly, like a dog casting off water. Why waste another moment of thought on the woman? He had a duty to do, one last task. So, he needed to report and see if he might somehow rectify tonight's error.

And yet, despite all, his thoughts went back to the Lady Cat, and his scowls fell away and his face softened in the dark of his carriage as he reconsidered the warmth of her kisses.

***

As Ian traveled toward his home, another carriage arrived before that stately abode. A man wearing a black domino and a mask that helped hide his hooked nose slipped out of its interior, reaching with nervous hands to raise the door knocker before him. He stepped back into the shadows as he waited, so the light from the windows did not fall upon him.

The door was opened by a butler, whose black clothing, stiff white shirt, and stoic face only served to agitate Georges all the more. "Your master? Is he to home?" he said, making an effort to pronounce the "h" sounds.

"I could not say, sir," the butler said with a cool formality.

Georges made a motion in the air before him, full of exasperation. When he spoke, his accent was more pronounced in response to his uneasiness. "'E is expecting me." *Not exactly.* "Is 'e 'ere, or no?"

The butler straightened even more than his already correct posture would seemingly allow. "When he wishes it, I will be glad to inform my lord of your call, if you would be so good as to give me your name, sir?"

Georges gathered his wits. He was not going to be admitted, and who could blame the servant? A masked man at the front door?

*I am become too visible,* Georges fretted. It had never been planned he'd go inside at the masquerade, but Lord Ewald, supposedly dressed as a king, had never appeared out of doors. And now here Georges was, at the man's very home.

"Please," he said, folding his hands together in a prayer-like gesture. "Please to tell the viscount, and only the viscount, my

55

message. This message, *exactement*! Tell him...," he hesitated, striving to find a message that would say all and yet very little to the casual ear. "Tell him 'ze cat has come home.' "

" 'The cat has come home,' sir?"

"*Oui*...yes."

"I shall do so, sir."

Georges nodded, staring at the door as it closed politely but firmly to him. These English servants had very curious ideas as to who ran the household, but there was something in this man's demeanor and in the sudden light of comprehension in his eyes that implied he would fulfill his charge as stated. *Bien.* "The cat has come home" was a completely innocuous statement; but *le vicomte* would know his duty was not yet discharged, that Georges's need was still great, that he had made his way to *le vicomte* despite missing him at the masquerade.

Georges slipped back into his hired hansom cab and ordered the driver to take him to a quiet part of town to find a room for the night. He only hoped his meager supply of English coins would hold out until he could, finally, come in contact with the designated Englishman.

***

As Georges' carriage pulled away from Lord Ewald's residence, a mounted rider urged his horse away from Viscountess Stratton's home just before she was helped down from a carriage of her own.

Now it was back to report to Lord Quinn, as he'd been ordered to do by that woman, Miss Lyons. The rider grimaced; he didn't care for Lord Quinn's newest compatriot. In point of fact, he might have pretended to lose sight of Lady Stratton's carriage as he'd followed her from his master's house to her own, out of spite. Quinn's hostess was sharp-tongued and imperious, whereas Lady Stratton *looked* young and innocent. But, too, given Lady Stratton's uninhibited laughter and garb this night, he could only assume she was of the kind that made up Lord Quinn's more private circle. God knew, there were those who liked the peculiar, wicked games of his master's sort.

If the rider had shaken his head and clucked his tongue to himself, mildly shocked to have learned the cat's identity, it was no bigger a shock than some of the others he'd had in Lord Quinn's employ.

***

Olivia went onto her knees, as she did every night just before taking to her bed, to offer up her prayers. For a moment she mumbled the words of the Lord's Prayer, but as she finished, it was not on the prayer her thoughts lingered, but on the feeling of arms around her, and lips upon her mouth.

She'd felt she should, but she couldn't really pray, at least not to forget or to be forgiven. She'd do it all again without a second thought. For it was impossible to believe she must deny the night that had awakened her once again to all the wonders of being alive. It was illogical to rue what she looked upon as a gift, a wonderful, glorious gift. The man's touch on her body had awakened every sense, every part of her slumbering soul, had reminded her life was for living, and that she was right to go out into the world if she wished to be a part of it. She'd been given a starting point, a new beginning, on which to build the rest of her life.

Kisses could be wonderful. A man could be intriguing. She'd been numb, but now she'd been kissed into awareness.

She laughed to think such silly thoughts--even as she thrilled from head to toe all over again. She closed her eyes, but it was a long time before the dark eyes foremost in her thoughts slipped into her dreams.

# Chapter 6

Phoebe sat back in the chair in Olivia's dressing room, watching her younger sister with contemplative eyes. Something had happened last night to Olivia; Phoebe was convinced of it.

There had never been a more dramatic change in a person. She knew she was completely right in thinking this, for even Olivia's little maid, that Mary Kate, had been disapprovingly watchful at her mistress's giddy mood this morning.

"What do you think?" Olivia asked Phoebe, each hand tugging forth the hem of a dress in her wardrobe for display. She had yet to change out of her nightclothes. "The rose, or the peacock?"

"Olivia, surely the peacock is an evening gown?" Phoebe cried, rather shocked.

Olivia cocked her head on one side, and nodded. She giggled, pulled down the rose gown, and reached to undo the ties of her nightrail.

Phoebe rose to help her sister. "You are gay today," she said, steering the conversation in the direction she wished it to go.

"Am I?" Olivia asked, throwing her sister a bright smile that acknowledged the fact.

"Why, one would believe you to be in love."

Olivia laughed again, merrily. "Oh no," she assured her sister, shaking her head and smiling as though at some private joke.

This was not missed by Phoebe, who was all the more intrigued. Nor had she missed that Olivia had said nothing toward the fact Phoebe had come to call, and so early. Good heavens, when *was* the last time she'd called on Olivia? But she'd been burning with curiosity upon waking, wondering why Olivia had been at Lord Quinn's masquerade. Once her children had been settled with nanny and tutor, she'd come at once.

"Do you know, it has been ages since we've gone to the market, or the shops, or had a *modiste* come to us," Olivia said as Phoebe finished with the last button on the rose muslin.

"Gracious, it has. Since Mama was yet with us," Phoebe confirmed.

"Do you have time to spare? Shall we go? Let's not wait for a *modiste* to come to us, let us go to her," Olivia cried, smiling at her sister's reflection in the cheval glass opposite where they stood.

"By all means," Phoebe agreed.

She didn't add that Olivia would have some trouble being rid of her until she got to the bottom of the mystery.

***

Olivia wasn't unaware of her sister's keen eyes upon her. She simply was unconcerned by the fact. Phoebe couldn't know what kind of an evening she'd spent.

Having such a rich secret was enough to make a statue grin, let alone a woman who not only could say she was young, but one who had begun to believe it again last night. She'd wanted to throw off the mantle of death and grief, and she'd done it. Now it seemed impossible she could ever have allowed the past to hold her back, pin her down, make her something other than she really was. She'd been living a lie, and it had taken some soul-blooming moments in the dark to make her not only reach beyond it, but know she *must* continue on her new path.

She knew exactly where she would start in this renewed life of hers: kisses. She would go out into the world, and she would flirt, and she would let men kiss her, time and again, until she'd had enough of kissing.

*It might be awhile*, she thought.

"Why are you smiling?" Phoebe asked.

Olivia shrugged, and tucked the smile away, not least because she wondered if all kisses were as affirming as *his* had been...

Phoebe handed her a fichu, intended to be secured around her shoulders and tucked into the front of her gown, but after a moment's thought Olivia put it aside. She was showing a little bit of décolletage, true, and it was morning--but her gown was not too daring. Phoebe lifted a brow, but she said nothing as Olivia retrieved a pair of walking boots. A quick application of a hairbrush and a twisted topknot was all Olivia was willing to do with her hair, but Phoebe must have found it acceptable, because she nodded.

A pair of gloves, a parasol, a reticule, and a cream-colored pelisse finished the ensemble in under five minutes, and the sisters stepped forth, out into the busy morning streets of Mayfair, toward the even busier streets of the fashion district.

Olivia knew exactly what she was going to do first: order another gown made. There were only three days left before she would need it, so she'd be paying a premium. On her tray this morning there'd been an invitation. It'd been from Lord Quinn, the sight of his distinctive spiky writing making her widen her eyes as she recalled all she'd done last night--too, it was odd to receive a second note from him, this man she scarcely knew. Was he a candidate for giving her a new kiss or two?

She might have smiled, but another thought occurred. Could he have seen through her disguise and known it had been she last night...? Did it matter? But no, he'd not known her at the fortune-telling table, of that she was sure. She'd sliced the wax seal on the envelope quickly, and had seen it was an invitation to a gathering to "Celebrate the Downfall of the Guy Fawkes' Gunpowder Plot of 1605, with Dancing." The date, naturally, was set for the evening of November Fifth. Another unusual party then, commemorating an old thwarted conspiracy against Parliament and James I. Olivia had glanced again at the invitation, mildly disappointed to see it was not to be a costumed affair--and had resolved at once to go.

So now she needed a new gown, something splendid, something to suit her true, unmasked return to society.

"So how did you spend your evening last night?" Phoebe called after her as Olivia charged ahead.

"Preparing for today," Olivia answered, amused anew by Phoebe's answering frown.

***

Kellogg, Ian's butler, rapped twice on his master's bedchamber door, and a recently roused Ian mumbled for him to come in. A footman had preceded the butler, having brought the morning tray. It straddled Ian's legs as he lay propped up in bed, its spread not yet touched.

"My lord, there was a caller last night."

"Yes?" Ian said, reaching for a toast point. Who would know to call on him? Sir Terrence? "An older gentlemen with a mustache, was it?"

Kellogg allowed a frown. "Younger, I would say. He was not of the sort to be admitted. He was in costume, his face covered. A foreign man. French, I think."

Ian rattled his tray and he almost dropped his toast, staring into the servant's face. Kellogg had been hired two weeks ago, and Ian had only met him with the rest of the staff two days since. None of them had been trained to respond to the pressures, and secrets, of a house given over to duty to the Home Office. Nor would they have to learn, once this business with the French informant was over.

"A French *man*?" Ian emphasized.

"Yes, my lord. He wished me to give you a message."

"Which is...?"

"'The cat has come home.'"

Ian made himself relax and settle back against his headboard. "I see," he said, giving his tone a dismissive quality. A keen light in Kellogg's eyes dimmed a bit at the master's indifference. "If he comes again, please admit him to the front parlor. Give him tea and food. I will see him upon my return."

Kellogg's interest sparked again. "If you are not to home, I should have him wait?"

"Yes, if he wishes," Ian said with the same unconcern. "But, yes, I would prefer it."

Kellogg nodded and bowed his way out.

Ian sighed. Nosey servants were always a problem. At least this would be a short-lived one.

Not that it mattered much, however. In fact, today was to be the beginning of his end as an agent.

But...a *man*? The informer *was* a male, not the female from last night? Ian had made contact with the wrong person; now he was all but sure of it.

Or could the man merely be a messenger? 'The cat has come home.' A man in costume, with an accent, coming to Ian's home, choosing to speak of a cat...

Either way, man or woman, what now? Was Ian to wait for further contact? Why hadn't the man shown himself last night at the masquerade? Or stayed here to meet with Ian at home? Certainly Kellogg had not granted the stranger reception or safety. Or had the man needed it? Was he in fact just a messenger, now done with his part? Not having seen the man for himself, how was Ian to judge?

Now, when it came to the woman, he had a better sense of her. If anyone had seemed in need, it had been she. In need of what?

63

Hiding? Then why dress so daringly? To be sure to catch his eye? Had she been in need of protection? Then why not go with him?

The way she'd kissed him, sweetly but hungrily, as if he were her lifeline... And what about the way she'd lost her accent?

Surely she *wasn't* the informer. Surely.

As he rose and dressed, Ian was mindless that he'd neglected to eat, and that he'd not rung for his new valet, Prentice. He'd served himself many times in his life, servants coming and going each time his family had traveled on, and with his last hired man in India having chosen to remain there instead of following the master he'd served for a relatively long three years. It was only when Ian was tying his cravat, poorly, that it occurred to him to summon his man.

"Prentice," he said over the hands that strove to correct the harm he'd done to the construction at his throat. "You're now free to let others of your acquaintance know who's hired you. Please have Kellogg inform the entire staff."

"Very good, my lord," Prentice said with a relieved look on his face. It must have been awkward to not name his new employer, but Ian had wanted to remain unspoken of until the masquerade.

He rode out into the day, to make good on two intentions. The first was thwarted. At the Home Office he'd asked for Sir Terrence, who'd not been in, and he was given a time to return tomorrow.

"So for now I must decide on my own what to do about the French informer," he murmured to himself.

Time to see to his second task. He rode to Bond Street, hailing the first person he came across, a gentleman in his fifth or sixth decade. "Good sir," he said, perfectly aware of his presumption. "I am a stranger to London and wondered could you direct me to a watchmaker?" He had no need of a new pocketwatch, but it was as handy a trick as any other to begin to know people.

Despite a scowl at Ian's temerity, the gentleman came nicely up to snuff by responding, "Certainly. Sir . . . ?"

"Ewald. Viscount Ewald."

The man's eyebrows lifted. "You are Aaron Drake's boy?"

"Even so," Ian replied, gratified for his father's sake that his name wasn't completely forgotten.

The man considered him for a moment, then belatedly offered a bow. "And I am Lord Broderring. I must say, does this mean your father...?"

"Has passed on, yes. Over four months past."

"Sad news. I knew him, in our salad days. Good with a cricket bat, I recall. My condolences, my lord."

Ian dismounted to return the bow. "Thank you, Lord Broderring."

"Wasn't your family in some foreign place?"

"Lately of India."

"I see. Well, lad, it is my pleasure to meet you. Your father was a fine man, fine indeed. You have his look. I should be pleased to show you the way to a very fine watchmakers."

"You are most kind," Ian said sincerely.

The older man served the purpose to a nicety, performing introductions as they walked, Ian's horse led by the reins. He was introduced to those persons known to Broderring. Ian nodded and smiled and bowed, cataloging names and faces as was his custom. In short order there were a dozen he could properly call by name.

He was no longer a stranger to London.

After pretending to evince some interest in a timepiece at the watchmaker's, and after a half hour of even more introductions, he made his sincere excuses to the older man who had done him such a kindness, and rode away toward Hyde Park. He looked for another not-too-blatant opportunity to introduce himself...but he knew he also looked for *her*.

It was ridiculous, of course. The Lady Cat had taken pains to hide her identity, even if she wasn't his missing informant. She'd meant to remain unknown, and he had no real reason to seek her out. If she was the sort to be invited to parties such as Lord Quinn threw, she was no manner of a good candidate as a wife for him, not to a man who might put a toe into a different kind of governmental pond, that of serving in the Upper House.

Still, there'd been polish in her manners, so surely it was possible she might be found among the members of the *ton* spending their morning strolling and shopping...? But, no, not really. Might she?

It was preposterous to bother to look... But look he did, even as he shook his head at himself.

His name continued to cause a bit of a stir. Many were, just as Lord Broderring had been, surprised to learn Ewald's heir had returned from climes afar.

"Do you have a house in London?" a pretty brunette, Miss Malcolm, asked him as she slowly spun her parasol over her shoulder.

"I do. I have chosen to reside in the old family home in George Street."

"And do you intend to remain in England permanently now?" She tilted her head, to look up at him with a slant of her dark eyes. *Dark eyes. This is not my mystery cat.*

"I do so intend, my lady." He would've had to be blind not to see the flicker of interest this claim created in the lady's gaze. He gave the young woman a second glance, idly wondering if she might prove to be the future Lady Ewald.

As his wanderings continued, Ian had to admit to himself there were other ladies who showed interest in his prospects, from misses to mamas--but none of them had the form or coloring of last night's lady.

He frowned to himself. He couldn't like that the lady--in his own mind, he'd begun to simply call her Cat--had caught his fancy so firmly. It was useless to ponder who she was; irrelevant. He was setting his sails toward a domestic harbor: he wanted a home, and a home wanted a wife. A man wished to take to wife a beauty who was sweet, and clever, and unique, and...

And who knew if Cat was any of those things?

A call interrupted his thoughts. It only took him a few seconds to realize here was a Charley, one of England's night watchmen, calling out the hour and naming the waning day as being All Saints. The early dusk of a cool November 1st night was chasing the last of the few intrepid park riders back to their homes. Though, he thought with a nod toward superstition, perhaps their defection was caused by the watchman crying out his warning that the ghosts of All Souls' were on their way. Ian smiled to himself, used to all manner of superstitions; there had been plenty in Turkey, India, and any of the other countries where he'd lived. For himself, he decided, he liked the watchman and his portents, and he smiled again as he thought if he was introducing himself to his homeland, it was introducing itself right back.

As he mounted and turned his horse, it was not toward home. Instead he rode into an obviously poorer part of town, one of those avenues of twisted alleys that every city hosts, and wandered into a smoky and thickly populated tavern.

"Good Publican, a round for the house!" he cried as he entered first the one, and in time several more. When asked who was paying, he always answered in a voice intended to reach multiple ears, "Why, it is the new Viscount Ewald, come to celebrate his homecoming!"

He stayed long enough to be seen sipping his ale, and to let it be known he was a convivial type. His purse was sadly depleted by the time he waved farewell to the day. Still, he was satisfied as he rode toward his home, knowing there would soon be no place in London, high or low, that would not know of his presence.

It was entirely possible he'd made the wrong decision by making himself so public, by not staying home and trying to remain nigh invisible--but, male or female, the informer knew where he lived. The plan had changed; there were no instructions; there was no point to his anonymity any longer. Either tonight or tomorrow, he'd find another message or else would be visited again, he was sure.

As he handed his horse to his groom, he was aware enough to acknowledge to himself that he hoped he'd have a visitor, and that she'd be a woman of light eyes and hair.

***

Georges shivered from cold, and hunger, and a need to relieve himself. He'd been waiting in the shared mews behind Ewald's home for *hours*. By God, where was the man? The loaf of bread Georges had stolen from a costermonger's cart was long gone. Twice he'd had to hide inside a large barrel and pull on its lid awkwardly, when others had brought horses to be groomed.

Ought he to dare the house again? Surely the butler would take another message? Yes, and Georges could leave his direction. Ewald could come to *him*, why not?

But then he flinched from the idea. What if Ewald's people were not trustworthy? *The butler, he must have heard my pronunciation, and the English, they do not love the French.* The man might be entirely willing to earn some coins by delivering a Frenchman to the *gendarmes...*

*Non.* His first plan was best: talk directly to *le vicomte.* The man could be caught alone between the mews and his home, *sûrement?*

Was there any other way? Anyone else to contact? There was a Sir Terrence in the Home Office... But where was that? What did Sir Terrence look like? Would he rebuff or even denounce a man who struggled to speak the English?

Grinding his teeth, Georges slinked away, knowing he must come back again tomorrow, under the cover of night, to see if Ewald was at home or could be approached when he returned from whatever evening outing.

***

Sophie poked her head into her mistress's bedchamber, and murmured, "Mademoiselle?"

Lisette Lyons came awake, immediately reaching for her wrapper. "Show him in," she ordered; at this hour it would be one of the operatives with which she worked.

He was ushered into her back parlor, his coat making a soft rustle in the quiet of the night. The man smelled of cigar smoke and ale. Lisette moved to a chair before the fire, shivering slightly in the night air. "Well?" she demanded as she sat.

" 'Is name is Ewald," he said in a round cockney. "The second Viscount Ewald. Proper name o' Ian Drake."

"You do not need that silly accent here," she said very quietly in French.

He obliged at once, his voice shifting to their mutual first language. "He has been around to the pubs, telling everyone who he is."

"Curious." She thought about that for a moment. "Did he meet with or speak of Lady Stratton?"

"No, mademoiselle. Although he did make a close study of everyone he met."

Lisette tapped a finger against her lips. "Why did they meet at the masquerade? Why did she go to the garden with him? I thought I knew what was happening--" She looked up at the dusty man again, and demanded, "Is that all?"

"That is all, mademoiselle."

"Then go." She reached into her bureau and extracted a silver coin, which she tossed to the man, to reinforce his nationalism with cold cash. He left with a bow.

Who was this Viscount Ewald? He was an English aristocrat; he could not possibly be the escaped Frenchman. Why had he gone to the tool shed with the disguised Lady Stratton? Why had the two of them left in separate directions?

And why had Quinn invited Lady Stratton, who had faked a French accent, not only to his masquerade, but now his Guy Fawkes soiree? Lisette had lost him as her lover, but Quinn still provided a great deal of protection to her. As his hostess, she was accepted, even admired.

She was not ready to give him up, not even if she were mistaken and there was nothing untoward going on. Certainly she did not wish another woman to take away any of his consideration. A man only needed one hostess, after all.

She turned to the bureau and extracted a piece of paper, a quill, and a jar of India ink. It was simple to write a love note, one calculated to inspire even the most timid of men. She did not even have to give it much thought, thinking instead of how soon she would find herself in Alexander, Lord Hargood's company, and consequently swept into his sister's company.

# Chapter 7

Ian was dressed the next morning by an attentive, talkative Prentice. He idly wondered how many facts he'd learned over the years from loose-tongued servants. How many of his own secrets had been innocently--or otherwise--given away because of servants's chatter?

Ian knew he was good at conversing without revealing... But all that was irrelevant now. He was a spy for only one more small thing, and that thing was hardly the greatest State secret. He scarce needed to trust his new servants, not under the obligation of duty anymore anyway.

He called upon Sir Terrence when he first rode out, and reported the target had yet to be secured. The older man was flustered, but Ian explained contact had been indirectly established. "I shall have him in hand by tonight, no doubt."

"Bad business," Sir Terrence growled. "I can't imagine how the fellow is getting on."

Ian had puzzled out that the informer was a man--but having the matter clearly affirmed somehow left him feeling flat. "Tell me, sir, are there other French persons in need of our assistant, in London at present?"

"What?" Sir Terrence asked, leaning forward. "None of which I know. Have you heard something?"

Ian waved the comment away. "Not at all. I have no contacts here but you. I was merely curious. As to curiosity, can you tell me anything of this informant, why he need flee England?"

"Very little. State secrets and all, you know. But I can tell you he is no supporter of Bonaparte. And in the past half year he has provided the location of important troops and their ordnance. His last report...well, let us merely say France is inflamed and a significant bounty is now attached to Douzain."

"That's his name? Douzain?"

"Georges Douzain. I risk telling you, that it might aid you, since the first contact point failed." Sir Terrence gave Ian a pointed look. "We owe Douzain a debt. We will take him far from the Corsican's reach. We need to have it known in the proper circles that our assets are protected. You must make contact with the man as soon as may be."

Sir Terrence instructed Ian to send a note to him at home once the informer was acquired, only then sitting back and inquiring how Ian was settling into his homeland. "And the home farm? Have you been there yet?"

"No, sir. But I will go soon. My father's steward has things well in hand, but he writes that he does wish me to come and see for myself."

"'Tis a good thing to go and meet the tenants, of course. Get yourself a wife, and they'll be glad for seeing her, too."

One side of Ian's mouth went up. He gave a single nod at the advice, which was in step with his own feelings.

"I want to say again that I'm sorry for the loss of the old viscount. Your father served his country well."

"Thank you. I believe so, too." Ian almost made to stand, but changed his mind. "Sir Terrence, might I ask an unimportant question?"

"Certainly. And I might answer." Sir Terrence smiled.

Ian gave a quick smile, too, at the old quip. "The man who threw the masquerade I attended, Lord Quinn? What can you tell me of him?"

"Ah, yes," Sir Terrence said, clearly not put off by the question. "A peculiar man. Strange beliefs. The Home Office is well aware of him."

"Is he at all trustworthy?"

Sir Terrence pushed out his lips and drew them in again, considering. "I wouldn't care to see my daughter marry him, had I one. He has peculiar ideas. His title is not old. His family name, Quinn, is the same as his title. His father earned the title through service to the Crown, although I could not give you the details of how that was shaped." Sir Terrence's mustache riffled up and down as he worked his lips again for a moment. "But, as for England? We are not concerned. We watch him, but I can assure you the man is a true patriot. We are confident he would take no action, knowingly, that would harm our fair land."

"But, surely, there is something...corrupt there? Something that could be used against him, or twist his honor?"

Sir Terrence shook his head. "In some ways, that is the strangest part of the man. He's some manner of nature worshipper--but nothing unfortunate, such as Satanism. Of this we're certain. He's curious, and highly intelligent, but harmless... Unless you've heard otherwise? Do you have anything new to tell us of the man?"

Ian measured his thoughts and impressions, and in the end shook his head. "I can only report that I found the masquerade...earthy."

Sir Terrence gave a small laugh. "Yes, I daresay. But not *quite* unsettling or distressing, hm? Yes, your conclusions are very like those often come to us on the subject of Lord Richard Quinn."

"Well enough, then." Ian gave a little lift of the chin, signifying both thanks and an end to the minor subject.

Sir Terrence wrote out his home direction for Ian's use, and stood. "Come along then, we'll nip 'round to White's, what do you say? I'll sponsor you, and see if you don't gain your place there in short order."

"Much obliged," Ian said, meaning it. To be selected for membership in the gentleman's club would be the final brushstroke on the art of his homecoming.

\*\*\*

Ian happily settled in the reading room of White's, a news sheet spread open across his knees, a snifter of brandy close at hand. Sir Terrence was talking racing in the corner with an old friend.

Trained to the task, Ian's ears buzzed from the various gossip, innuendo, and small talk around the room. He learned Prinny had won a weighty wager on his latest cross-country carriage race, but that was no surprise, as the Regent was often allowed to win. He heard that an organization called the London Society of Beefsteak Admirers had been founded just a few houses away, and apparently lived up to its name. Of course there was much said about the abolishing of the trade monopoly of the East Indian Company; those were dark conversations, for there were to be losses, no doubt some of them fortunes.

All of it was intriguing to Ian, who was used to being at least a continent away from the center of the empire, and consequently weeks if not months behind on anything but the local news. To hear it so new, so fresh, to be a part of the central unit, news pouring out as it happened or was delivered to London's ears, was exhilarating. It only reaffirmed his desire to stay, to learn more about this nation of his birth.

Would he miss the art of surveillance? Perhaps. But he would be contributing to his nation's well-being in a whole other way. He would work to be a good steward to his land, to his people. He could play a part in the House of Lords. He was ready to be a landowner, a man charged with bringing forth produce and employment. He listened to the prattle about crops and weather, a subject newly important to him.

Too, there were those who merely wanted to gossip about their acquaintances. That was not to say such conversation was not just as absorbing. Ian learned that Lady Rendell was living in a separate residence from her husband, with a young "nephew"--whose blood relation was highly suspect. There were tales of royal tomfoolery, of riches lost to wagering, of the loss of respect in young persons these days as evinced by Sir So-and-So's comments to Lord Some-and-Such, and, of course, the inevitable tales of romantic trysts and foibles.

Ian might have copied the gentleman sitting to his left by closing his eyes and drifting off, but a new name caught his ear. The title "Lord Quinn" was spoken between two younger men. It was the easiest thing for Ian to raise his news sheet as a shield, with his ear pointed toward their quiet words. It was amazing, really, how little people believed their voices carried.

"Are you going?" the first man, tall and thin, asked the second, his expression somewhere between temptation and doubt.

The second, not as tall and with a rounded face, hedged. "Are you?"

"My cousin said he'd bring me along, if Quinn's willing." His voice had lowered even more as he'd said Quinn's name. He flashed a look around the room, Ian saw as he turned a page of his news sheet. "No costumes this time. I'd like it rather better if there were masks again."

"I don't know about it all. I've heard...stuff goes on, later."

"What'd'you mean?" Now the thinner man leaned forward to catch every word.

"I heard...it's just said...that is, that sometimes not everyone is....all clothed." This last was said very quietly, so that Ian could not be absolutely sure he'd heard correctly.

"Women?"

"And men!"

The thinner of the two gave a hissing sound, somewhere between shock and titillation. "I don't know, Ollie. Seems...peculiar-like."

"Some say--" Ollie cut himself off.

"Say what?" his friend urged. His insistent tone overcame his friend's resistance. "Some say he's a devil worshipper," Ollie said.

A silence fell, and the young men considered the shocking claim.

"Did you see that one woman?" Ollie asked.

"Which one?" Robbie asked.

"The one dressed up like a cat."

Ian suppressed the impulse to lean forward into their conversation.

"Oh, yeah. What about her?" Robbie said.

"I hear she's Quinn's newest interest. At the masquerade he predicted she'd have a lover soon. They're saying he meant himself."

"Is she a devil worshipper, too?" Robbie asked, something like awe in his voice.

"I dunno. But she was luscious, wasn't she? Dressed up like she might not mind the stuff that happens after proper folk leave, I say."

"What? What kind of stuff?"

"Weird ceremonies," Ollie said, his voice going quieter and quieter. "Half-naked dancing. Orgies."

"What're orgies?" Robbie asked.

"God, you're such a simpleton," Ollie scoffed.

Ian rose as Ollie labored to explain the term to Robbie. Folding his paper and tucking it under his arm, Ian made his leisurely way toward his sponsor. He bid Sir Terrence farewell, thanking the man and saying he hoped to join him here as a member one day. He left a nodding Sir Terrence to the chess game in which he was now entrenched, tossed the newspaper on a tabletop, and struck out for the street.

*Quinn, a devil worshipper. And Cat, a naughty temptress.* Interesting gossip, indeed.

Ian had been too long abroad, though, in many places where he'd seen and heard tell of any number of alarming practices, to be unduly disturbed by such accusations. But it was rather unexpected that rumors of devil worship and orgies were whispered of in the heart of the so-called civilized world. These might well be but mere claims between two foolish pinks--but Ian knew rumors ought not be discounted out of hand. Especially not when he'd seen the excess of his host's decorations and costuming for himself.

Perhaps an acquaintance with Lord Quinn--and, through him, the elusive Cat? who was more and more sounding less like any sort of woman to be taken to wife, Ian acknowledged with a scowl--was something to be pursued...

***

When Ian returned home he was met by Kellogg, who delivered the day's post into his hands, among which was a missive from his brother, Arthur. Ian's heart lifted. How had any letter from Arthur found him so quickly?

He put the letter in his coat pocket in order to listen to Kellogg tell him that one of the chambermaid was leaving his service to care for her sick mother and that another girl was being sent by a respectable agency. Further, that one of the footmen had found evidence that someone had been sleeping or hiding in the mews.

"'Someone'?" Ian echoed.

"Daniels, the groom, said a barrel was tipped on its side, and there were bread crumbs and footprints inside. It was most probably a one-time thing, my lord. Some vagrant. No cause for alarm. But if we catch anyone, of course I'll send at once for the Watch--"

Ian held up a hand. "Didn't I ask that anyone coming to call be put in the parlor to await my return?"

"Calling, my lord, yes. At the house. But not in the mews, surely?" Kellogg must have realized his questioning was cheeky, because he immediately added, "I didn't realize you meant anyone, house or no, my lord."

"And of course, no one was actually found or seen," Ian admitted, considering for several long beats. "Kellogg, tell the lads that if they can get their hands on anyone about the house or grounds, to bring him in, here, and we will give the stranger food and drink. Put him in the back parlor, or if he seems too rough, bar him into the pantry. But try to treat him well enough. I wish to speak with him." Ian began to walk away, but paused to add, "Hold *anyone*. A man, or a woman. With or without a French accent." He would not share the man's name with the servants, not unless he had to by some chance.

"Of course, my lord," Kellogg said with an apologetic bow and allowing only a hint of questioning to show on his face.

Surely the intruder had been the informer. Damn.

Ian went to his room. Arthur's letter was brief but good news. His ship had docked in London for a few days, and the first thing he'd heard was that the new Lord Ewald was in residence. Arthur was to call tomorrow.

Ian went up to the room that had once been Arthur's--he recognized it when he mentally added a bed and a wardrobe--happy he would get to share the return to this house with his brother.

The thought of Arthur's visit made him restless, however, so Ian went back down the stairs to reclaim the beaver hat and gloves Kellogg had already brushed and set on the cloakroom table.

"You are leaving, my lord?" As servants could, Kellogg put a wealth of inquiry into the sentence.

"I shall be back for supper," Ian assured the butler. He didn't need to report his comings and goings to his man, but it amused him to answer.

"Do you require a horse or a carriage, my lord?"

"A horse."

"Very good, my lord."

"Kellogg, wish me well." he said, donning his hat.

"Because, my lord?"

"Because I am going to the devil."

# Chapter 8

"Ah, I thought I did not know you when my man gave me your card, but I see I am mistaken," Lord Quinn said as soon as he had crossed the threshold of his own receiving room. Both residing in Mayfair, it had taken Ian not even a five minute ride to return to the house that had hosted the masquerade.

Ian stood from the seat to which he'd been shown, bowing in greeting. The wide-shouldered Lord Quinn ought to have appeared quite different, now dressed in perfectly ordinary garb, but even the fine cut of his coat and pantaloons couldn't hide the specter of the man who'd dressed as Samhain. There was something... predatory about the man, in costume or not.

Lord Quinn half-bowed in return, clearly reserving a fuller reception, and crossed the room to make a gesture indicating Ian should sit once more.

Ian returned to his well-appointed chair. Along with taste, the furnishings made it evident Quinn had a plump purse.

Lord Quinn lifted his chin toward Ian. "I know your face. You were Louis XIV two days ago. But it's only because of your calling card I now know your name, Lord Ewald."

"That is why I came to call, to thank you for your delightful party. Too, as there were no announcements, in the end I was remiss in not introducing myself. I must tell you, too, I was there under false pretensions. Sir Terrence gave me his invitation."

Lord Quinn's eyes narrowed, but otherwise he did not evince any upset. "I wondered."

"I am newly returned to England, and Sir Terrence was kind enough to let me use his invitation in order to enter English society a bit more slowly than at an unmasked affair."

There was no change in Lord Quinn's expression, but there was an attentive attitude to the way he sat, his hands too neatly folded together, like coiled snakes. "You have a hint of an accent. You have been abroad, my lord?"

"For years. Turkey, India, Germany, Italy, France." This last was said with no particular inflection, though he looked directly at Lord Quinn as he spoke. He saw the large frame, the steady blue eyes, the firm, large hands. This was a powerful man, both in size and in demeanor. It was, on the one hand, easy to take him at face value as the average English gentleman, the sort to be more concerned with hunting than attending the House of Lords--but on the other hand, it was also easy to imagine this man could be the kind to do as he chose, hunting down a far different manner of game than mere fox or pheasant. This was a man who could be a worshipper of darkness...or a man who might grant aid to one who had informed against the French. Without knowing him, it was impossible to say which, if either, was the more likely.

Yes, this was a man to get to know, regarding the informant...and, perhaps, regarding the Lady Cat.

Ian chose his strategy, but there was also sincerity in his tone. "I have realized that I and Sir Terrence have overstepped. I have defied etiquette twice, once at your party, and now by introducing myself to you. But I must tell you that everything about your masquerade has persuaded me you are a man who can live outside a rule or two, and that you might tolerate my cheek." Ian stood, crossing his hands behind his back and bowing his head. "I offer you my apologies, for invading your home and for my forwardness. If you reject me now, I will fully understand, but I am hopeful we might further our acquaintance."

Lord Quinn merely tilted his head a little. "Why?"

The question surprised Ian, but then he allowed a smile to slide across his face. "Because I find you interesting."

Quinn considered that for a long beat, while he also stood. For a long moment longer Ian suspected he'd been too obvious, had spoiled his chances for further acquaintance.

"And I find you refreshing," Lord Quinn said at last. An eyebrow quirked upward. "Presumptuous, bordering on rude, but refreshing nonetheless."

Ian's smile widened. He drew a card from his waistcoat pocket and held it out to Quinn. "Please feel free to call upon me. My direction is on the back."

Lord Quinn escorted him to the door, and they made their *adieux*. As Ian stepped out the open door, Quinn considered him for another long moment, then said, "Welcome to England, my lord."

"Thank you." Ian hesitated, deliberately, though he hoped it didn't look that way. He half-turned back to Quinn. "Perhaps I shall enjoy my time here more than I'd at first thought, my lord."

Quinn put one hand on the door, stepping back. With his voice devoid of any intonation, he said, "That is to be hoped, my lord." He then quietly closed the door, leaving Ian to stare at the solid wood for a moment before he turned to find his carriage.

As he rode home to his bed, Ian couldn't be sure if he was anywhere near to completing his duty, but he had done what he could to lay the groundwork for an introduction to at least one version of London's underground society, if Lord Quinn was indeed involved in such. What that underground involved--hidden fugitives, or brazen masqueraders, or satanic rituals?--remained to be seen. He could do no more now than wait to see what grew from the seed he'd planted this night.

\*\*\*

Lord Quinn turned from the door, moving to Lisette's side when he saw she'd come from the sitting room to join him in the hall.

"Richard, what do you zink zat was all about?" she asked softly. She stood near him as he shrugged silently, but did not lean into him, for she had learned how quickly the man could anger at what he would read as an insincere demonstration. Where feigned sexual allure was a tool easily used with some men, it was a disaster with Quinn. She'd been his lover for a short while, but it had been nearly a miscalculation on her part, and had quickly cooled on his. Thank God he found her intelligent and liked her discourse.

But being no longer his bedtime pet was as well in the end, for Lord Hargood had responded just as she'd thought he would to her note, making an assignation for tonight. There was no way Quinn would have ever shared the favors of a woman with another man. But now she'd even told Quinn she was taking the young man as her lover; he'd made no protest. He was unusual in that he could remain a friend to a one-time paramour. Good thing. His home and his name were excellent protection for a woman who could not hide her accent. Never mind it niggled Lisette's vanity that Quinn was so plainly unmoved she'd gone to another's arms.

She was very, very careful to make sure he didn't know she was a Napoleonic loyalist, for that would be disastrous. Lord Quinn was many things, but first and foremost the man was an English patriot, strange as that fact might seem to others who didn't really know him. He wouldn't hesitate to turn her over to English authorities. If he came to know she betrayed him with every missive she placed into sympathizing or purchasable hands, she wasn't entirely sure he mightn't strangle her to death with his own hands.

When first she'd arrived in England, she'd needed a patron, as soon as possible. Not just anyone, but someone who presented the opportunity for blackmail, for that was the surest way to control a man, to get him to do things he normally wouldn't do, or to keep his mouth shut when normally he'd talk. She'd heard the rumors of Lord Quinn's darker side, and he'd been therefore a natural choice. Her accent was not as troublesome as others might think, for there were many French refugees in London. She scarce stood out. It should have been a simple thing to trap him, but she'd learned otherwise; the man had his peculiarities indeed, but he was also centered in iron, not one to be the victim of extortion. Too, the man and his beliefs were well-known to English leadership; he'd protected himself by befriending well-placed men and by being utterly open with them. If there was anything to blackmail him with, it was unknown to Lisette.

Her usual skills useless here, instead she'd substituted a more intimate relationship, that of the mind, echoing his own sentiments, following his lead. It had served as well for her purposes as her more usual temptations did not. How it served Quinn was his own counsel, for he had given her no clue by which to judge, although he'd been amenable to making her his official hostess.

Now he belatedly answered her question, just as softly as she'd spoken. "The man is some manner of spy, I venture. While there is a hint of an accent in his voice, I do not find that extraordinary. It comes from his years abroad. But I do wonder, does he serve two masters?"

"The government," she repeated. "And?"

Lord Ewald had come into Quinn's orbit at the same time Lisette had learned a traitor sought refuge from French justice. Ewald had secretly met up with the costumed Lady Stratton. For herself, Lisette believed the "and" was: Ewald or Stratton's responsibility for aiding the traitor. Or both.

Quinn went on, "You believe there is some connection between this man and the Lady Cat?"

"Lady Stratton," she reminded him of the name she'd learned that night. So he'd made a connection there, too? Quinn was both observant and clever, and she only played one game with him, that of hiding her truest intent to help France. In everything else, she told him all. "You know I saw zem, together, enter ze dark shed. And was she not using a French accent? Zat must have been, surely, some kind of signal. Of course I believe zere is some connection between zem."

"But you could not see their actions in the shed, could not hear their words?"

"No. But, what else but to trade secrets? To share passion? Pah. The English know zis," she snapped her fingers, "of passion."

He turned back to her, smiling with his mouth but not his eyes. "Oh?" he asked softly.

"The English women," she corrected swiftly. "Zey are raised to be the hothouse flowers, pretty to look at, but do not dare to touch zem."

Quinn turned back toward his study, giving no sign whether she was to follow or not. She trailed him, but the gap between them grew.

"I have touched many a hothouse flower," he said over his shoulder as he reached the door. He paused long enough to add, "I believe I will invite this Lord Ewald to my Guy Fawkes affair. He was certainly angling for an invitation. I will oblige him. I would learn more of the man."

"And what of Lady Stratton?" she asked, looking for and finding the expected spark of regard that leaped into his eyes. Others might have missed this sign of interest, but Lisette had not.

"Oh," he said slowly, almost smiling, "Lady Stratton has been invited already." Then he looked directly at her, his expression benign. "My dear, won't your lover be expecting you soon?"

She managed to keep her face passive until he closed the door between them with a gentle click, but then her eyes narrowed to slits. She knew a dismissal when she heard one. Perhaps it was as well she was making an alliance with Lord Hargood; she must be prepared should Quinn ever look at her truly askance, or take a notion to dismiss her as his hostess. Perhaps that would be for the good, as Lord Hargood was not nearly as sharp-witted as Lord Quinn. She turned with a swish of her skirts, calling for her cloak in an impatient voice.

***

Olivia crawled into bed, content with her day's activities; today she'd ordered new pelisses and spencers to go over her bespoke gowns. She'd also ordered new kid slippers dyed to match the deep emerald satin of the gown she'd been promised would be ready for Lord Quinn's party. She knew exactly which jewels she would wear--the emerald and pearl pendant, with the matching earbobs. Her newly purchased gloves were of satin, pearly white to match the jewels.

"I think you ought to ask yer sister along," Mary Kate had said when Olivia had told her of the Guy Fawkes evening of dancing.

"The one advantage of being a widow," Olivia had told her maid, "is the lack of need for a companion or chaperone." As Mary Kate had pursed her lips, Olivia had thought to herself that she'd go to Quinn's party three nights from now, be polite, watch her laughter--heaven forbid she be identified by it so soon after the masquerade--and enjoy herself, as herself, as she had not done in ages.

Her mind flashed to the note on her dresser, a missive penned by her brother. He'd written that, since he owned his own box at Covent Garden theater, she should join him the night after Quinn's party there. Unusual as his inclusion was, it was even stranger when he offered to escort her "elsewhere, as needed."

Whatever did "elsewhere, as needed" mean, especially when Alexander wrote it? Had he had an awakening of family feeling and meant to spend more time with her? That remained to be seen.

She'd sent a note in return, her first impulse being to refuse on principle of prior neglect and uncertain motivations now...but then she'd decided she wouldn't mind in the least the chance to take in a play, as it had been ages since she'd last enjoyed such a treat. So, instead, her return note had affirmed the date; the greater future could be handled through the expediency of never mentioning her plans to her brother. Had he seen her at Quinn's masquerade? She hadn't seen him. Otherwise, she couldn't think why Alexander suddenly wished to escort her about, but she'd take advantage of his offer as it suited her. What better way to reenter society than just to go and do it? And why not with her brother, who, say what you would, could be counted on not to introduce her to rackety people.

The same could not be said for those who'd also be attending Lord Quinn's party, she thought with an indulgent smile. She'd have no mask to hide behind this time. Neither would she hide behind Alexander on that occasion. But she would certainly put herself out to seem engaging. She might even flirt with Lord Quinn. Or any man who amused her. How else was she to gather kisses?

But...what if she saw *him* there? The idea of kisses brought her King Louis very much to mind.

She forced the thought of dark hair and eyes aside, lulling herself to sleep with thoughts of the sparkling conversations she would have at the celebration, primarily with Lord Quinn, who would--she grinned at her own hubris--be fascinated by the young widow.

However, when her imagination reached beyond and into that liberating time when nighttime fancies slide into dreams, gradually the figure in her sleep-ridden thoughts was no longer Lord Quinn, but returned to a golden-clothed Louis XIV.

***

Alexander settled back in his bed with a sigh of deep contentment, for a pair of delicate arms were wrapped around his neck, and a pair of soft, pretty lips were nibbling at his earlobe. Lisette made a soft murmur, one that brought a contented sigh to Alexander's own lips.

"Will we meet tomorrow?" she said near his ear.

He sighed to have the mood disrupted with talk, but he gave her an answer. "No. I'm sorry, my dear, but I am occupied tomorrow. In fact I cannot be with you for the next few days."

"Oh, Alexander, never say it is so!" she pouted prettily, rising up on one elbow to look down into his face. "Where do you go that I may not?"

"Well, m'club, of course. But tomorrow I'm engaged to do a spot of rowing on the Thames. There's a bit of blunt on the line, and I mean to win my share. Then the lads are meeting afterward for a game or two of whist. Then, there's supposed to be a smacking good racehorse to be had at Tattersall's on the fourth, he's won every race he's run so far. The day after that, if I buy the beast, I've got to see him put through his paces. The day after *that* I'm committed to view a bout of fisticuffs at Gentleman Jim's, with perhaps a cockfight after. The following day, I'm off to my banker's, and in the evening I agreed to see my sister to the Theatre Royal. So you see, there's nothing for it--"

"Oh, Alexander," she sighed, her tongue back at his ear, teasing, flitting, warm. "What a fine brother you are. Is zis ze older sister?"

"Phoebe? No, Olivia. You might know of her? Lady Stratton."

"Ze widow?"

"That's the one. She's coming out of mourning. Got to see to her, as a dutiful brother must, of course."

"Of course. So you go with her to see Mister Edgemont at ze theater?"

"No, my box is at Covent Garden, not Drury Lane."

That was where the small talk stopped and kisses renewed--because Lisette had already learned which theater she'd "coincidentally" be at four nights from now.

# Chapter 9

Three nights later, Olivia posed before Mary Kate. The maid had dressed Olivia in all her finery, her hair swept up and held atop her head with pearl-studded pins. Mary Kate still disapproved of Lord Quinn, but even she had trouble insisting there'd be danger in a roomful of unmasked members of the *ton*, or that Olivia's emerald gown was improper. It fit well and suited Olivia's coloring, and showed a perfectly correct amount of bosom. Her emerald and pearl jewels glistened at her neck and dangled from her ears, and her mirror and Mary Kate's nod told her she was in fine form.

This time Olivia rode to the occasion in a crested carriage, wanting the world to know who she was. She was not overly concerned her newfound boldness would slip. No, those days were behind her. To go back would be to place one foot back in the grave of all those she had lost in too short a time. She could not do that, never again. She had grown, and now could face life as a woman, not as a frightened girl. She would be daring and bold and never retreat.

Her determination lent her an air of calm, so that when she descended from her carriage, she entered Lord Quinn's graceful home with a regal bearing that advanced the knowledge to the world of her determination to hold her true head high.

She was announced. Some few heads turned at the sound of her name. She could almost hear their thoughts: this was the Viscountess, Lady Stratton?

Olivia stepped forward, offering her gloved hand to her host. For a moment Lord Quinn's dark blue eyes danced, until they were obscured as he bowed over her hand. "How pleased I am you've come tonight," he said as he straightened, looking at her directly again.

"How pleased I was to be invited."

"You were also invited to my masquerade, but did you come? I don't recall seeing your lovely face when it came time to remove the masks."

Olivia hesitated, but then decided there was no harm to come from confession after the fact. "I was here, dressed as a cat."

There was something in the way his eyes glittered that told her perhaps this wasn't news after all. "Ah yes. The tarot predicted your future."

"Which has yet to come true."

He smiled, a man's smile at a woman. "There is time."

"Indeed," she said, looking away from his penetrating attention, and then another partygoer was announced and she moved on.

Really, there had been warmth in that gaze, a not utterly unpleasing warmth. This could, no doubt, explain why the man was a popular host--if he looked at other women in this same intense, almost hungry way, and despite his reputation for dissolution. In fact, her eyes had gone to his hair, almost expecting to see the Samhain horns still there, and had been mildly disappointed to find it was not so. There was something about the man that made him seem even more in disguise without the horns or the outfit, as though his fine black evening clothes were the costume, not the other way around.

She moved into the room, pleased to recognize some ladies from her widow's groups and church. A longtime acquaintance, one Mrs. Dennis, moved toward her.

"Lady Stratton! How delightful to see you here tonight," she called.

"Mrs. Dennis, it's lovely to see you, too."

Mrs. Dennis, bless her, pulled Olivia into a group, making introductions. Thus ended any openly curious stares at the long-missing lady.

Mrs. Dennis turned back to Olivia. "But, my dear, what brings you out this night?" Her speaking eyes went on to say that even when they'd met before, never had Olivia looked so sophisticated or polished. When and where had the girl gone, leaving this refined woman in her place? said her expression.

"I have come to enjoy an evening out," Olivia answered simply and truthfully, the bright smile that accompanied the words causing the ladies around her to smile along.

Olivia had been ready for denouncements if they were to be forthcoming. She knew she was fair to look upon, with a monetary worth that only added to one's attractiveness. She'd dressed with care and a bit of dash. Her brief prior season had taught her some women considered any other woman to be competition. But instead of rejection--and perhaps because her daughters were all married--Mrs. Dennis merely asked to know the name of Olivia's *modiste*.

As Olivia supplied the information, which led to a discussion of the latest trend toward exaggerated epaulets for riding habits, internally she shook herself, a silent sigh of relief coursing through her. She'd done it. She'd shown the world her true face, and had been accepted. Her head almost spun with the giddiness of the moment, with the release of the weight of isolation she'd been carrying, needlessly, foolishly, for far too long.

A group of gentlemen came up to the ladies, a few of them inquiring as to availability for dancing. Gentle laughter rose as agreements were made. Olivia looked up, catching the eye of the gentleman nearest her...then over his shoulder, some twenty feet away, she saw the man she knew only as Louis XIV. She gasped aloud.

\*\*\*

It had become perhaps only a bit of a parlor game, after all these years, for Ian to memorize yet more names and faces. Besides, he already knew a third of the others also attending Quinn's celebration, by reputation if not having actually met them yet. Quinn's Guy Fawkes party was not so highly attended as his Hallows' Eve masquerade had been; this seemed a gathering of more intimate acquaintances, to judge by the ease of conversation between them and by the smaller numbers.

Quinn's home was large, and boasted the previously used ballroom, half of which was now unlighted and cut off by a row of tables, since fewer attendees needed to be accommodated. The half-room now lacked any harvest plenty. For decoration there were only clusters of Union Jack flags, and a couple dozen kegs of varying sizes set about the room, over-representing the explosives with which Guy Fawkes and his compatriots had hoped they might blow up Parliament. The ostentatiously oversized charge cords lay about, meant to seem "ripped out", as though the Gunpowder Plot had not only been found out, but rendered inert.

Ian's brows lifted. Lord Quinn's decorations were not those of a nihilist, but a loyalist. Was this meant to mislead, or did the Home Office have the correct measure of the man? But perhaps he ought not draw too firm a conclusion, because, after all, what manner of fool would have public decorations that *supported* chaos and ill will?

The festivities began, in that guests were directed to tables from which to select tidbits from small plates. Everything was petite, a bite or less, clearly meant to stimulate, not satisfy the appetite. Too, while there were at least a dozen delicious selections to choose from, the item count was low; latecomers would find only empty plates. In all his travels, Ian had not seen a like food offering. He was coming to find Lord Quinn the sort to surprise on many levels.

He traded tidbits for a glass of sparkling wine. It was not champagne, Ian noted, even as he considered that champagne would have had to be gotten from smugglers, a highly illegal act in these days of war with France. Another sign of patriotism? Or mere cost-savings? As illegal as smuggling was, Ian doubted that fact alone would have stopped Quinn from getting what he desired.

Thinking a man must be judged through his acquaintances as well as his actions, Ian scanned the crowd a second and third time--but he couldn't deny he was also looking for a specific lady. With a lowering sensation, he acknowledged he didn't see anything to make him think Cat was among the invitees.

*Truly, it's time to cease looking for her*, he chided himself. That night had been an anomaly. To waste anymore time or thought on a few stolen moments was folly. He was no callow youth to pine after a woman he didn't really know.

*Think about something else...* So he thought about seeing Arthur earlier in the day. It had been--there was no other word for it--*wonderful* to see his brother again. It had been too long, yet the bond was still there. They'd toured the house, sampled from a half-dozen of Papa's severely dust-covered bottles from the wine cellar, and traded memories. Arthur had too few from their time living in the house, but when they'd gone through those limited few, and on to ones from their mutual youthful travels, Arthur had then regaled his brother with tales from his time at sea. Arthur had done well for himself, sitting there so resplendent in his Lieutenant's uniform. A naval life clearly suited him.

The visit, though hours long, had been too short. Arthur had left with the promise to return whenever he was fortunate enough to take port in London... Ian's fond recollections were interrupted by his ears catching a French accent.

Eyes flying to the source, he located an attractive woman in a pale blue gown. Her hair was up, several braids ending in an artful woven knot, and was of a light brown color. *Cat's hair might have been a very light brown.* Ian's heart skipped a beat. In the glow of the overhead chandeliers, as he stepped closer, he affirmed this woman's hair could be called as much blonde as brunette, highlights glinting in a way that made his lips part in response.

He'd attached himself tonight to one Mr. Connell, a baron's son he'd met that day at White's, and turned to him now. "Connell. The lady in blue? Who is she?"

Mr. Connell nodded in the lady's direction. "That's Miss Lisette Lyons. Lord Quinn's hostess." He leaned in to add in a whisper, "It's said they used to be lovers, but no more." He stood upright again. "I can introduce you, if you like."

Ian considered the woman, knowing that, yes, he'd seen her before. He realized with a touch of disappointment that she'd been dressed as a harvest gleaner, and had very much acted the hostess for Quinn's masquerade. Had she also worn a cat's costume for part of the evening?

It wasn't impossible... He also saw she was no more than five-and-twenty, but still old enough Ian wondered that she'd not married by now. Her accent might supply an answer, especially if she'd escaped France without family or dowry. Not to mention she kept unusual company.

Ian listened to the sound of her voice as she spoke, even closing his eyes to try and hear if this was the voice he'd heard in the dark five nights past. The accent made it harder to say. His first thought was the voice was not the same, but when he opened his eyes and looked again upon the woman's height and general demeanor, he was not sure. Surely Cat had possessed a slimmer waistline?

Too, he must remember the woman in the darkened shed had lost her accent. This woman's was lighter, perhaps a reflection of some months, if not years, spent in England?--but it was also possible this Lisette Lyons's accent could be more pronounced when she chose for it to be. Under the influence of their shared passion, Miss Lyons might have forgotten to stress her accent. If it had been passion. If her accent was real, as he thought it might be. If it had been Mademoiselle Lyons at all with him that night.

When he heard her speak again, he was yet unsure.

When he saw her move, it was the same. Her figure was all that ought charm the eye...was it her dress that made her ribcage seem broader than his hands had told him Cat's was?

However, all his careful consideration went flat as she turned her eyes toward his: brown eyes. The Lady Cat hadn't had brown eyes.

More logic struck him: she was already established here in London. Comfortably so. What possible need would this lady have to be relocated, to be gotten out of England?

Unless something had gone terribly wrong with this re-established existence of hers, she could not be the one. She was not the informant...but was she the Lady Cat he'd held in his arms so recently?

Not with brown eyes, she wasn't, he reminded himself.

Disillusionment swam in his belly, even while he admitted, again, that it was folly indulging his fancy like this.

Mr. Connell moved to a new group, and Ian let himself be pulled away from the attractive but disappointing Miss Lyons. Still, he noted when Quinn came to gather Miss Lyons for the first dance. Here, too, was another clue; she didn't quite seem to move like the cat with whom Ian had danced.

He looked around to find the lady, a Miss Comstock, to whom he'd committed his first dance of the evening.

The dance over, Ian relocated Mr. Connell, pulled forth another social smile, and stepped up to the small group of ladies Mr. Connell had joined. He gave a bow to Lord Quinn, who'd also stepped up, and to each lady as Mr. Connell presented them. "Mrs. Carlyle. Countess Montgomery and her daughter, Miss Eulalie. And," Mr.

Connell turned in the remaining lady's direction, "this is Lady Stratton." Ian let his eyes linger a moment on the very pretty stranger as his own name was pronounced. Then his smile faded, for she was looking up at him with shock on her face.

"Lady Stratton," he greeted her, putting a question into it. He felt a bit flustered by her open-mouthed stare. Ought he know her from his travels? He wasn't used to forgetting faces, if he'd done so.

"Lord Ewald," she murmured, still staring even as she curtsied to him.

A jolt went through him. There was no French accent, but that voice...! He searched her being from head to heel. Red-gold hair, leaning more to the gold. Those green eyes. A tiny waist...

"Cat?" he breathed out.

Her blush told all.

He couldn't help it, he moved toward her, one hand poised to take her arm. Only at the last moment did he check the publicly unwarranted advance, turning it into another bow, deeper this time.

Those searching eyes... The shape of her chin... Yes! Yes, this was the lady whom he'd kissed and fondled, who had kissed and fondled him back. The lady whose sigh against his lips had been so unexpected and so delectable.

"Ladies," Mr. Connell had gone on, "Lord Ewald is recently returned to us from India."

"India? Oh, how fascinating," Miss Eulalie purred.

Ian had to force his gaze to shift to the young lady, even as he took a half step back to include the other ladies. Absently, he answered in the negative Miss Eulalie's question as to whether he had plans to return to India. His eyes flicked back to Lady Stratton, to see she now stared fiercely at the carpet. *I'm giddy,* Ian thought, absolutely shocked to know it was true. *My God, she's a beauty.*

Music struck up again, and Lord Quinn offered an arm to Lady Stratton. "My dance, I believe." He'd granted her the second dance, just following on the heels of the first with his hostess.

She went with the man, only glancing at Ian for a second before she was taken away to the dance floor. Ian couldn't have said if the glance was seeking information, was an apology, or begged him to say nothing--but he resolved at once he'd be her next dance partner, regardless of who else had first sought the privilege.

*Here is Cat! She is found.*

He stayed near the couple, observing them obliquely as he sought and received answers to his many questions from those among whom he stood: she was a widow, having been married to an old man. Newly out of mourning. She resided yet in a London home she'd shared with her husband, although it had returned to her, via some grandparent's legacy, after her mate's death. Her deceased mother had been fortunate in her wealth all her life, leaving the daughter funds not attached to any entail, and Stratton's will had left her a proper widow's portion, so Lady Stratton was far from destitute. The title and Stratton Hall, in Hertfordshire, had gone to her husband's heir, his grand-nephew, but it was said the two weren't close and the man seldom came to London. The new Lord Stratton was unmarried, so his grand-aunt by marriage had yet to have "dowager" attached to her title.

Her Christian name was Olivia.

Ian silently tried the name on his tongue, slowly displacing "Cat" with "Olivia."

So then, this Olivia, Lady Stratton, was no French informant. She was a well-to-do widow, and a bit of a cipher to their present society. The latter description not unlike Ian himself.

The music concluded, and he was at once at her side. "Lady Stratton, might I have the next dance?"

She hesitated. He hung on her answer, his heart in his throat as it had been when, at age sixteen, he'd first asked a woman to dance with him. *Why am I acting like an over-eager puppy?*

She silently replied with a nod, and Ian let out the breath he hadn't known he was holding.

Lord Quinn had turned aside to others, as a host must, but he'd not moved far from Lady Stratton's side. Now he slid a narrowed glance at Ian, but his expression otherwise hid any deeper meaning. Quinn slid his arm under Olivia's hand, an old trick, but a successful one as he led her away for the short time until the musicians were to start up again.

With a little time for observation, Ian fell back on trained pattern. The agent in him saw who had a tendency to over-imbibe, who had an eye for the women, who gave out the most cutting gossip. Too, without Cat-- Lady Stratton's innate glow directly filling up his gaze, his eyes could see servants were discreetly scurrying as though readying for a party, though their efforts made no change in Quinn's second floor ballroom that Ian could see. That was peculiar, for Lord Quinn had not supplied gaming or card tables, and those gentlemen who desired a cheroot were out on the balcony, in plain sight of the dancers, their need for port or cigars already seen to. He couldn't believe Quinn was having his staff begin disassembling a party still in the making...?

The aroma of further cooking was scenting the party, and that seemed a trifle odd, too. As Ian had conjectured, the edibles that had met the attendees were all gone, with no servants replenishing the platters. As soon as that was clear to him, it was furthermore obvious that a dozen or better partygoers knew it as well as himself. They were the ones who grouped together, their eyes occasionally finding and evaluating the servants's burdens.

He looked around the long room to find Lord Quinn, the man's large frame bending down toward Lady Stratton, apparently making some kind of inquiry of her. She was smiling up at Quinn, and Ian wondered how he couldn't have known her for even a moment. A rather immature dash of jealousy flashed through him; was her smile warm? What did the lady think of their host? This was at least the second time she'd been in Quinn's company. Were they familiars? Ian frowned.

However, he was not so distracted by his conjectures that he failed to notice some of the partygoers were slipping away. Some nodded thanks over their retrieved cloaks and hats, evidence they were leaving for the evening--but others seemed to disappear further into the house, presumably to some back room.

It wasn't until the leave-takers were bowed out that the first strains of a new tune were practiced. Ian made a direct line toward Lady Stratton. It was clear as she looked around that the busy servants had caught her attention as well. When she spotted Ian, her color deepened, and something leaped in his chest.

Was she invited to whatever was to come? Was everyone? Did the beautiful, seemingly somewhat shy young widow know what was coming next? Ian watched her tongue run between her lips, and wondered if it was a response born of appetite, or uncertainty? Was she a devotee of Lord Quinn and his ilk? Or, by way of an assumed accent, was she an innocent, accidentally caught up by in events beyond her?

# Chapter 10

Olivia tilted her head, offering her ear to Lord Quinn. A polite smile framed her mouth as she leaned toward him to hear his words over the general hum of conversation around them. Truth was, though, her mind was across the room.

*Lord Ewald. His name is Ian Drake, Viscount Ewald.* What she'd done with him, how they'd touched, how *alive* she'd become in those few, wonderful, impossible minutes... *Here I am, in the middle of a ballroom, and all I can think is I want to slip away with this Lord Ewald and do it all again...*

She'd no more than formed the improper thought than Lord Ewald marched up and offered his hand to her.

She took it, looking up to find that his eyes searched her face. He'd brought forth a smile now. Ought she to smile back? It seemed...wayward, after her thoughts, so she kept her mouth a straight line. *See what comes of wanting excitement in this life...*

She took her place opposite him, glad they were not to share a waltz this time. Glad, too, that he'd released her hand, for she'd been afraid he might feel the heavy beat of blood through her veins there. The tunings stopped, the other dancers fell into position, and the music began in earnest. It was a country line dance, involving skippings, genteel claps, and changing partners.

*He knows me! That it was I who wore the cat costume. What can I possibly say to him? Ought I flee and not even face him?*

When they came back together, Lord Ewald spoke. "Is all well with you, Lady Stratton?"

The question startled her. "What do you mean, my lord?"

"The last time we met, I thought you were," his smiled widened, but somehow not unkindly, "a damsel in distress."

Olivia considered how to answer him. Would he censure her for her misbehavior that night--or try to repeat it? He couldn't possibly think her a decent sort. So why not the truth, since he couldn't think much worse of her? "I was looking for adventure."

It was a moment before he danced back before her. "It was certainly that." He smiled again. "I normally wouldn't question a lady, but why 'adventure'?"

She sighed, looking down at their moving feet. "Four years of mourning. Papa. Mama." After a moment, she added, "Stratton."

"Ah," he said, traces of humor dropping away. "You have my condolences. I, too, have lost family. My parents."

"And a wife?" It was an insensitive question, but he'd started the exchange.

Lord Ewald shook his head. "I've never married." It was his turn to pause a little, but then he went on. "That's why I've come to England, actually. To marry. To grow crops, and children. And old."

She gave a shaky smile at the little joke. *He's come to find a wife...*

They were silent for a few moves of the dance. Olivia reminded herself to breathe; it would never do to fall faint at the man's feet. When his hand touched hers once more, he spoke again. "My lady, I wonder if I might call upon you at your home? If so, what days do you receive--?"

The music ended rather abruptly, and they both turned to see Lord Quinn had waved the musicians to silence. A quick glance told Olivia that only four sets of dancers yet remained in the room; all others had left, though a distant buzz of conversation and moving feet made her think not all had gone from the house. In fact, if pushed to say, she would have guessed from the expectant smiles of the others that of the eight dancers, she and Lord Ewald alone were not old confederates well known to Lord Quinn.

Their host spread his hands. "To those few of you who are unaware, let me inform you I have asked some of my close friends to stay on a bit tonight, now the dancing is come to an end." He glanced around at the eight dancers, but his gaze settled on Olivia. "I hope I am not too presumptuous in asking you to stay?"

"Do we play cards?" she called out, a stall as she considered if she wished to stay, to have to answer Lord Ewald's inquiry, or if a very quiet, very safe evening of tea shared with her maid held more appeal.

It certainly wouldn't hold as much uncertainties and curiously compelling moments.

"No," Quinn answered her. "We partake of a late-night meal." He paused, then added, "In a manner to my preference." The other dancers, already moving to join Quinn, tittered; yes, they were familiar with the man and "his ways."

The taller Lord Quinn looked over their heads to catch Olivia's eye. She nodded her agreement to stay. Pleasure wreathed his face, and he came toward her. Olivia was acutely aware of Lord Ewald at her side, his hands folded together behind his back, his expression inscrutable.

"I am most pleased you choose to stay. And you, Ewald?" Olivia didn't see if that gentlemen nodded or not, but Lord Quinn presumed by going on, "Excellent!" He gave his regard fully back to Olivia. "But first we are to have a grand march, after which I ask that you sit at table, on my left. Do you please?"

"A grand march?"

But Quinn rushed on again, leaving her question hanging. She turned to Lord Ewald, who shrugged in answer to the dangling words, and offered her his arm instead.

They followed Lord Quinn to where some twenty others were, indeed, gathered a floor below, in a back parlor.

Crossing to a clear space before the hearth, Lord Quinn held up his arms again to gain everyone's attention. When they'd fallen largely silent, he made his announcement. "Let us, please, assemble by twos and make our way back to the front doors." Lord Quinn, taking Miss Lyons on his arm, smiled, his teeth gleaming in the candlelight. "Do not disdain to make a great deal of noise, for I shall consider this a poor affair indeed if tomorrow my neighbors make no complaints to me."

Intrigued laughter rippled through the room as the crowd fell into pairs--Lord Ewald retained Olivia on his arm--and they lined up behind Lord Quinn's advance to the doors, where a bevy of servants scurried to return cloaks to their rightful owners. She had to release Lord Ewald's arm then, because the participants were also handed bells of various shapes and sizes, either on a handle or a length of leather, so that both hands were full.

"The church bells used to ring on this day in celebration that the House of Lords was not destroyed, so we must make enough joyous sound to rival the old custom," Lord Quinn told them.

Really, she thought as they stamped through the city streets, Lord Quinn was quite clever. Certainly anything but boring. When had she ever gone on a grand march? It was all silliness, of course, with the gentlemen vying with one another to make the largest whoop or whistle, and the ladies ringing their bells as loudly as they may and stomping their feet. Several persons had brought champagne glasses with them, and one couple recklessly ruined their host's property by dashing the two crystals together to create a jarring smash. One lady gave forth snatches of operatic arias, and many giggled or laughed aloud. Some of the men, a bit into their cups, waved the few lamps they'd brought in a reckless manner.

Their racket caused drapes to twitch aside, doors and windows to open, and despite the late hour a few children to emerge from the houses, begging a penny for "the Guy." Olivia had no funds on her, at least not until Lord Ewald pressed some coins from his purse into her hands. She threw them to the children, who hooted and shrieked and scrambled after the rolling coins, and she laughed with them.

Catching the spirit of the moment even more, and once the pennies were gone, Olivia clapped her hands together in way of making her bells jingle, half to continue to make noise as requested, and half to salute the group of revelers for daring to be so vulgar in the streets of Mayfair. She marched along, finding the evening invigorating--not least because of the man she was so aware of at her side.

She slid her gaze sideways. She was not surprised to find him looking down at her, but his expression was not what she expected; any smiles gone now, he was definitely considering her, and not necessarily in a kind light.

Her amusement seeped away. "You look as though you have a question," she said, perhaps a bit primly.

He gave a little *moue*, silently acknowledging she'd been correct. He lifted a hand, indicating the people around them. "You find this pleasurable, Lady Stratton?"

She glanced around as well, then nodded. "I do. Do you not?"

"Isn't it all rather…pagan?"

She laughed at him then. "Oh, surely it's harmless."

"Are you a confidante to Lord Quinn?"

There was definitely something disapproving in that question. "And if I am?"

Someone yelled out that their celebration was flagging, so Lord Ewald absently shook one of the bells he carried. "I see you take offense. Pardon me. It is just that I am...curious. I am trying to understand you. And him."

The words softened her a little, but she did not completely release her pique. "Are you the sort who cannot give himself over to simple enjoyment of a moment, my lord?"

He thought, and shook his head, as though to banish a thought. Then his lids lowered, and perhaps a hint of a smile came across his lips. "Why, no, my lady. I believe I'm capable of giving myself up to the enjoyment of a night." He stepped nearer, almost touching her.

So abruptly reminded how they'd met, Olivia blushed so deeply she was sure he could see her face darken despite the meager light. Worse yet, his reminder ought to have made her angry. Instead, the woodsy scent of his soap reached out to her, washing her anew in poignant reminder of the very memory he hinted at. She could not escape the thought of his lips caressing her skin in places that had never been caressed before, not even by her husband.

"If you will excuse me?" she gasped out, telling herself she owed him nothing and need not suffer any censure from him... And telling herself that moving quickly from his side was a choice, not a defense against her own insensible inclinations.

***

Unaware of a scowl on his face, Ian watched as Lady Stratton rushed straight to Lord Quinn's side. The large man turned to her as a flower turns to the sun, and Ian's scowl deepened. She was speaking to the tall, broad-sholdered man, and he was bending down his head to listen, even as they both continued to ring their bells with the crowd as they walked. Lord Quinn smiled at her--a warm smile even from this distance.

*Good God, I am jealous,* Ian admitted to himself, shocked to find it was true. *I don't even know her. Except her kiss is tender. Her aspect is gentle. Everything she does is touched with poise and intellect, even when she answers my rude questions...*

108

Very deliberately, he turned his attention, settling on Miss Lyons. Working his way to the front of the column of marchers, he came to her side where Quinn had given her his back in favor of attending to Lady Stratton. Miss Lyons turned to Ian, at once chatty, perhaps covering up the fact she was vexed by Quinn's neglect.

Lord Quinn's smile continued, Lady Stratton on his arm now, as he led his guests down Upper Brook Street and circled them back toward his home. The crowd laughed and pointed when one man called down from his bedchamber window "Enough of this nonsense, then!" But at last they'd come full circle, and the twenty or so men and ladies made their way back into Lord Quinn's abode.

Their host passed through the house, where their bells were surrendered but not their coats, for Quinn led his celebrants on out to his garden. At its center, Ian took in the piled wood and brush and the figure atop it all, and knew in an instant that the stuffed shape was an effigy of Guy Fawkes.

A servant brought Lord Quinn a torch, which spit and hissed as he handed it on to Lady Stratton, urging her to do the honors. Miss Lyons looked on with seeming approval, and most people--who could be amazingly unobservant--might not notice her smile was thin.

Lady Stratton was game enough for the task, and stepped forward to set the bonfire alight. The brush, unmistakably with the scent of lamp oil to it, went up with a gratifying *whoosh*. The gathering cheered and clapped their hands.

As everyone admired the dancing flames and the poor stuffed Guy was overtaken by smoke and fire, Ian watched as Lord Quinn touched Lady Stratton's elbow to draw her back from the flames as soon as she'd handed the torch back to the servant. He didn't let go of her arm. "Did you enjoy my march, Lady Stratton?" Ian heard him ask.

"I did," she said. "I must compliment you, for you are very clever at entertaining your guests with novel celebrations."

He bowed his head in acknowledgement of the compliment, and after observing the fire for awhile, offered her his arm again. She placed her hand on the sleeve of Quinn's heavy coat, and the two of them moved to the open doors, behind other couples also straying away from the gradually subsiding bonfire. Ian offered Miss Lyons his arm. She nodded, accepted his arm, and they fell into step near Quinn and Olivia.

Lord Quinn slowed his steps significantly, which Ian matched, still eavesdropping. "I must explain something to you," Quinn said to Lady Stratton. Ian paused, as though to half-turn back to admire the bonfire again, Miss Lyons not protesting at his side. Perhaps she was eavesdropping as well.

Olivia signaled by a lifting of her eyebrows that Quinn should go on, a silent acknowledgement his tone had turned serious.

"There will be an invocation before dinner, and it will no doubt sound a trifle peculiar to your ears."

"Indeed?" Lady Stratton--Olivia, *how I fancy her name*--seemed to hesitate a moment, but then she laughed. "Just when I thought I was getting used to your decidedly unique approach to matters, you always present more for me to consider."

"This is true. For instance, before we proceed I would have you understand that I am not of the Church of England."

Her brows rose. "A Catholic then? A Methodist?"

"No. But yes, I am after a fashion all of those. And more. You see, Lady Stratton, I believe in all the faiths."

Ian turned his head to give an unneeded cough, observing Quinn's face as he did, and saw the man's gaze was for no one but his current companion. Quinn looked down at Lady Stratton from his far greater height with the fixed attention of either a swain or a zealot. *Which are you?* Ian wondered, not quite allowing a frown to form, trying to maintain the ruse that he couldn't overhear them.

"Hinduism? Buddhism? Judaism?" Olivia asked.

"Yes, all of them."

She wrinkled her nose at her host, letting him see her skepticism. "You have made a study of all faiths, my lord?"

"I have. Every faith made known to me."

*What a truly different sort this fellow is,* Ian thought. He'd almost missed Quinn's answer, so now he turned himself and Miss Lyons as he murmured a reply to the latter that, yes, the night was growing more chill. He again matched his pace to Quinn's slow one.

Perhaps Olivia had also needed to consider Quinn's peculiarity, for she was silent for several long moments as they strolled. But then she spoke aloud. "That tells me something of why you have such a great tolerance for the unusual."

Quinn came to a complete halt, and the look he cast her all but glowed, and not from the bonfire's flickering. "Indeed. Indeed! How perceptive of you to see it in such a light. You delight me with your ability to temper your opinion of me."

"Do I?"

"You don't seem to judge me a lunatic, as so many others do once they know a bit more of my philosophy."

She blinked several times. "Perhaps I am merely polite?"

Quinn laughed, as Ian would have done in his place. "Oh, you are that, but you also are a woman of self-possession. You do not let others do your thinking for you."

She seemed to think otherwise, but then she nodded briskly, and something in her thoughts made her stand a little taller. "Yes. That is quite true."

"I am glad I spoke to you then, for you shall have the comfort of knowing beforehand that the meal will be a trifle unusual. I shall have the comfort of knowing you will not be unduly taken by surprise."

She might have argued that point or asked if her opinion was so important to him then, but instead Ian saw she merely gave a reserved nod.

Quinn led everyone back inside, into the dining hall. His guests were divested of their coats, and fell to mingling around a long formal table, which was set for a meal. Ah, so the prior gathering's meager foodstuffs had indeed been meant only to pique the appetite for this more formal meal. The room hosted a fair amount of potted plants, and was fair on to being gloomy, because the candles of only one small chandelier were lighted above their heads and only two torches- -one of which had surely been used to set the Guy ablaze--flickered in brackets above the grate, unusual, moody, and smoky. The high ceiling was completely lost to darkness, and shades and shadows nestled in the room's corners and danced among the potted plants, so that it was easy to believe one was to feast in some forest glade, with wild animals or masked men hiding just beyond sight.

*What fanciful thoughts,* Ian noted to himself, verging on feeling displeased. The agent in him cast his eyes about, acknowledging a growing sense of unease. Did he see Olivia shiver? And if he did, was it a reaction similar to his, or was it from keenness for the subtly disquieting setting? Was there menace here, and if so, did she sense it? Was she one of those women who thrilled at the hint of danger?

Or was it just that Ian wished she'd stand at his side and not Lord Quinn's?

He almost startled when he refocused his gaze and found hers fixed on his. Certainly it felt as though someone had poked him, for their eyes asked the same question: what manner of evening had the two of them agreed to?

# Chapter 11

Miss Lyons released Ian's arm and glided to Lord Quinn's side, as the hostess ought for the meal service. Olivia stepped to the seat on his left, as he'd requested, and took a moment to really identify her co-diners. As sheltered as her life had been, she was yet able to say here was a duke's mistress, there a man known for his licentiousness. Across the way, a man whose three duels had reached even Olivia's house-bound ears. And further down the table, there sat a woman known to smoke cigars and wager extravagant sums.

None of which made them any lesser than society overall... But she couldn't find a face among them that had been neglected by the rumormongers, and it put a tiny frown between her brows to find herself among them.

Although, there was one who was, so far, untouched by known scandal: Lord Ewald. Not an hour since, she'd been annoyed with him, but as he took his seat to her left, she found she was glad he was there. She was not the only "outsider" in attendance.

At the thought, Olivia looked up to find Miss Lyons staring at her, the woman's face coolly arranged. Olivia managed a one-sided smile at her, hoping to change the moment, but the only effect it had was to make the woman sniff and look back to their host.

Olivia thought perhaps she blushed; so the woman had noticed Lord Quinn had paid a fair amount of attention to Olivia. She squirmed in her seat, then stopped the motion, determinedly staring straight ahead at the salt cellar, arranging her face to reflect she had no concerns. Lord Quinn's behavior was no fault of her own.

Because she looked to the table top, Olivia belatedly became aware that but a single goblet sat near her plate. There was something odd about it. Not only were there usually several wineglasses in place, to be filled as the meal's demands dictated, this single goblet was filled with brownish water. Curious.

Lord Quinn rose at his end of the table, his hands folded in front of him. The room fell silent, as the dinner guests looked to him.

He cleared his throat and said, "As most of you know, I claim that it's not enough to say a simple, let us say, classical prayer over a meal. I believe it not only fitting, but requisite, to thank so much more than does the average Englishman. I maintain that, were our people more familiar with their own past, they would follow my lead and understand more clearly the nature of our existence upon this blessed earth."

Olivia looked to Mr. Turrell, seated on Miss Lyons's right, but the young man's attention was on his host. He was clearly undisturbed by the unusual pronouncement; Mr. Turrell had heard the like before, obviously.

Olivia couldn't keep herself from sliding a glance at Lord Ewald. He was sitting calmly, hands folded in his lap, and would appear the embodiment of polite attentiveness by his expression--until he met her glance for the merest moment. She returned her gaze to Lord Quinn, fighting an urge to smile. No, she wasn't alone here.

Quinn went on, his hands rising as though in search of a benefaction. "Great Earth Mother, known and beloved of the Druids, Keeper of the Fruits and Grains, Bestower of the Bounty, hear our cries of thanksgiving. Know we accept your labor, O Great One, the benevolence of the soil, the flesh of its creatures, into our bodies, to be one with thee, to complete the cycle of life and death, and life again! We know the fire that consumes the tree log is grateful for its

114

life, even as the tree is grateful for the fire that burns away the choking underbrush. The earth is obliged to the rain that falls upon it; the rain celebrates the earth that forms to hold the rain as streams and lakes, so that others, man and beast, might drink of the waters of heaven. We forget not the sea, Giver of Fish and Transportation and Beauty. Know, Great Mother, how vast is the appreciation of Thy servants, gathered here this night, we who wish only to serve the advancement of Thy great and wondrous intentions. Bless those who are new among us, and let their eyes be opened, that they may see the way to the joy and understanding Thou hath given us, that harmony in all things may, we pray, be achieved."

Quinn reached for his goblet, as did the others at the table without hesitation despite the peculiar-looking liquid, and that was when Olivia realized the goblet must hold well water. "A toast!" he cried. "To the Earth Mother, and to our special guests tonight."

"A toast!" cried the others as they raised their glasses toward Lord Ewald and herself. Miss Lyons's glass only lifted the once, toward Ewald.

Olivia reached for her own glass as she glanced around, mindful of the lack of trepidation the others displayed. Olivia had only had well water a handful of times, from estates built outside London. It had been drinkable, but the taste of dirt had been marked.

Lord Ewald seemed sanguine as he lifted his glass in a returned salute and said, "Ladies, Gentlemen, to your health."

"To your health," Olivia echoed.

The water tasted exactly the way she remembered and expected it to, but she could see how one could get used to it.

As Lord Quinn resumed his chair, Miss Lyons rang a small silver bell, and a stream of servants came suddenly through a door, carrying steaming trays of food, trays of wineglasses that quickly replaced the water goblets, and a plethora of wine bottles. The ceremonial water had served its purpose.

When the first course of a delicious leek and pear soup had been set before her and a glass of wine poured, Lord Quinn called her name. "Lady Stratton, you see we partake of not only the waters of the earth, but also the juice of the vine," he said, lifting his own red-filled glass in a salute.

"My lord, it is clear to me that you--" she glanced around the table with a carefully noncommittal face, including others in her glance-- "are interested in the practices of...I believe they were called the Druids? But, can you tell me, whoever is the Earth Mother?"

Gentle laughter surrounded her, but Quinn waved it away, signifying no offense was meant by the amusement. "My dear lady," he said, looking at her with approval. "I knew you were clever enough to know us by name. We are, indeed, followers of the ancient ways of the Druids. We gathered here--plus some few more who couldn't be with us tonight--worship the All-God, whom we refer to as the Earth Mother. Among her many names she is also called Life-Giver, and the Great One, and the Goddess. She is mother of all things, all beliefs. A way of looking at it, perhaps, is that Earth holds all the people on its face, regardless of their nationalities and practices, just as the Mother, the goddess, encompasses all gods, all faiths, all peoples."

"I see," Olivia said, picking up her fork to cover her ever-growing bemusement. "So...," she said, then hesitated, only to decide to go on, "so, you do not believe in God?"

"The Anglican God? The Moslem God? The Lutheran God? My dear, such fierce and regimented gods, the kind that repudiate one people over another, calling one better than the other. I believe they are all parts of the same whole god."

"Zeus, too? Apollo, and Cupid? And what of Thor and Odin and Freya?"

"All of them. Every one from the time when man first attempted to put a name to the forces that make up our lives," he said, his eyes alight, his tone that of a preacher who was encouraging a curious child.

"And what form does your worship take?" a voice interjected. It was Lord Ewald. Olivia turned to him, relieved to have him join the conversation, for her mind was buzzing. She'd never heard, never suspected, such society existed, and now she found herself in their very heart. One part of her wanted to rise and ask for her carriage at once to return home, where everything was just as it always had been--but there was another part, too, that wished to hear the answer to the question Lord Ewald had just asked.

Lord Quinn turned to him, but now some of his benevolence slipped just a little. "We pray," he said, staring into the other man's eyes. "We meet once a week for the Sabbath. We dance. We sing. We praise nature, for it is the embodiment of one side of our Mother. Other than that, we do little enough. We are a benign organization of like souls."

"No ceremonies, my lord?" Ian pressed. "I believe the Druids used to throw live cats into fires, and sacrifice goats. Do you enact any of those 'traditional' activities?"

Lord Quinn sat up straighter. "Only symbolically. Such as our march tonight. Though I won't say there is never a sacrifice made, but, think, a cat or a goat is also of the Mother, and therefore undeserving of cruelty. If an animal is butchered, then it ought be done humanely, by a skilled laborer in the art. We insist upon such reasoned acts."

Ian inclined his head, acknowledging the concept. "I believe clothing was optional at the Druids's ceremonies, as well. Is that true among your fellows?"

The room fell silent. Quinn put his palm to his face, resting his elbow on the arm of his chair, the posture meant to be relaxed, where his voice was not. "Why do you ask?" he said softly.

Ian looked around the room at the tight faces, and then shrugged elegantly. "I am merely curious. I have lived in many lands, some where every inch of a native's person was hidden, others where near all is exposed. I am not so shocked by, let us say, some people's need to feel less restricted than others." He turned toward Olivia, speaking mostly to her as he said, "My apologies, my lady. Ladies," he included the others seated around the table with a glance, "for the indelicacy of the conversation."

She nodded that the apology was accepted, for she was beyond words. A woman, leaning forward in her chair farther down the table, eyes avid, murmured that no apology was necessary.

"Lord Ewald," Quinn replied. "As I say, our group is made up of like-minded persons, but that is not to say we all practice our faith identically. I leave it to the individual to decide what part clothing plays in exercising their beliefs. Which, if you consider, is not unlike most people, whether they go to church or tabernacle or temple."

Lord Ewald inclined his head. "I cannot argue your point."

Olivia noted a few fleeting smiles, and once again turned her eyes down to the table. She did not even slide a glance toward Ewald.

The meal proceeded, as normally as might most any other late-night meal. To Olivia's relief the conversation turned to ordinary discourse. She spoke with Lord Quinn, but in deference to Miss Lyons's attempts to entertain the man, she chose to soon look across to Mr. Turrell, who, encouraged, regaled her with a tale of one of his hunting exploits.

Manners--and Olivia admitted the obligation matched her own inclination, despite her irritation with him earlier--meant she must include the other diner near her, so she turned to Lord Ewald. "My lord, I know your parents are no longer with us, but have you any family in England?"

"After a fashion. Arthur, my brother, is a Lieutenant in the Royal Navy. But he seldom is free to come to London."

From his tone, it was easy to see he wished it was otherwise. Olivia looked down at her plate in order to slice some beef. *A lack of family interaction is something we have in common,* she noted. *That, and being strangers among this gathering. And,* she glanced up into his eyes and found him considering her with a frankness that unnerved her a little even as it thrilled her, *an undeniable attraction, at least on my part.*

He dropped his voice. "Might I ask you a personal question, my lady?"

"Yes." She was not, however, obliged to answer.

"Why do you come to Lord Quinn's affairs?" Her eyes must have widened, because he went on. "You are not of their ilk. Or do you seek to be?"

She almost rebuked him, but he'd been her protector several times tonight, and perhaps he'd earned her answer. "Freedom," she said. "Life. These people are..." She cast a look about the room. "They are unique. They are decidedly alive and awake, whereas," she sighed, "I'd been sleeping."

He stared at her, not with censure but rather as though he truly evaluated what she'd said. He gave her a slow smile, transforming his face from manly handsomeness to something more that tugged at Olivia's inner being. That mouth...it knew how to smile. How to commiserate. How to be part of melting her time-frozen soul...

He lifted his wineglass in her direction. "We are both coming into new lives, my lady. A toast, to a kindred spirit," he said, lifting the glass toward her, where she'd belatedly raised her glass in kind. His words warmed her more than did the wine. A kindred spirit--was that why they'd been drawn together that night of the masquerade? Why they seemed to always end in each other's company?

Her gaze wandered beyond him, to the end of the table. Lord Quinn was looking directly at her, over the rim of the wineglass he swirled with deliberation. She looked away, a little startled to note he was upset with her.

The moment was interrupted when a syllabub, made of jellied blackberry wine and sweet cream, was brought in as the final course. Its stately wobble as it was wheeled in on a cart caused Mr. Turrell to make a comment comparing it to their overweight Regent, so that even Olivia had to smile just a little. After all, an insult to a royal was hardly the most astounding thing about the evening.

After the treat had been consumed, Miss Lyons set aside her spoon and stood. "Let us withdraw to the women's salon," she said to the ladies around the table.

Olivia could not help herself; she flashed a quick glance at Lord Ewald. She'd fled his side earlier tonight, yet now she was loath to leave him. He met her gaze levelly, and leaned forward to say quietly, "We'll meet again after the port."

She nodded at him, and trailed somewhat reluctantly after the ladies as the men pushed back their chairs and stood, preparing to find spirits and cheroots.

As she stepped onto the threshold of a parlor Miss Lyons had designated as the women's room, she couldn't help but gape. *Now why should this shock me, after all that's gone on tonight?* she asked herself, almost amused. The room was like no parlor she'd ever seen. It was lined with shelves stuffed full of old, thick tomes. Scattered among them were oddities: jars of liquid that held suspended some insect or small creature; bunches of herbs tied with ribbon or hanging from the overhead ceiling beams; small boxes with labels that read *borage, lemon balm, rue*, and more. An assortment of vials and glass jars were lined up on a large, thick tabletop, and sheets of paper, quills, and inkpots were scattered over the surface, giving the impression someone had just left their work to attend to some other pressing matter. There was the look and smell of an apothecary's shop.

"Richard's research," Miss Lyons said, taking up Olivia's hand and pulling her into the room. "Richard" being Lord Quinn, of course. If Miss Lyons yet resented Olivia, only the tightness of her fingers on Olivia's gave any sign of it now.

Servants had arranged a hotchpotch of chairs around the fireplace, the nine other women looking to Miss Lyons. She released Olivia to settle in a high backed chair of dark leather, her hands folding in her lap as she gazed at the assembled ladies. "Now, as to refreshments, what complaints do we have today?" she asked, reaching for a book that was on a small table near her elbow.

Olivia quirked her head, puzzled, but then another woman spoke up.

"I still have that ache in my knee when the weather is cool, as it has been."

"Alfalfa tea for you zen, my dear. Let us have it brewed from the seeds rather zan the leaves to see if zat will increase its potency for you."

"I am still weak. My heart, my disposition," a Mrs. Sedley exclaimed. "So I suppose it should be bark of the cherry tree tea for me again."

The other ladies nodded.

"I have quite lost my cough," another said with a smile.

"Ah, was zat from use of ze kerosene, turpentine, and pure lard poultice?" Miss Lyons asked, with a hostess's smile.

"No, it was the heated mutton tallow and lavender."

The other ladies murmured approvingly.

"Is zat all our concerns, ladies? Excellent. Let me just ring and give our requests to ze staff. While we wait, would you mind, Clara, reading to us from where we last stopped?" She handed the book she'd been holding to a young woman settled on a footstool next to her.

"Let me see," Clara said, opening the book and scanning the pages. "Ah yes. If you recall, we were partway into the relief of colds." She cleared her throat delicately and read, "'Solution the First. Make a tea from the leaves of boneset. Drink the tea when cool, not hot, as it will make you ill taken so. Leaves may be dried for winter use. Solution the Second. Put goose-grease salve on chest.'"

The ladies tittered at the use of the body-part word, but Clara didn't blush or stammer, reading on. "'Third. Eat onions roasted in ashes. This is good for children as well. Fourth...'"

She read on as Olivia's eyes flicked around the room. As nearly always in Lord Quinn's universe, everything was slightly odd: the room's stillroom-like *accoutrements*, the ladies reading medicinal receipts from old books, the ordering of unusual teas--none of which was peculiar in itself, but placed altogether they near to made the hairs on the back of Olivia's neck stand up. Perhaps it was seeing the preserved creatures? And the many scents not blending well in the close air? Twice she parted her lips to say she believed it was time to go home now, but twice she bit back the impulse, not wanting to offend. Really, what harm could come of any of this? And after all, wasn't she the very same lady who had promised herself she would never be retiring and missish ever again?

Clara read until a tray was carried in, with three separate teapots upon it.

Miss Lyons poured for Olivia, without consulting her.

Olivia hesitated over her dish of tea, but then decided even if she was made to sip at an alfalfa brew, surely it would not be such a terrible thing, for the other ladies accepted their various teas with no demur.

To her relief, her first sip informed her that her serving had come from a pot filled with perfectly ordinary Ceylon tea. She glanced over the rim of her cup at Mrs. Sedley, who made a little grimace every time she sipped her cherry bark tea, and gave thanks she was not required to do the same.

When the tea had been consumed, and the subject of poor Princess Caroline's latest sartorial faux pas exhausted, Miss Lyons rose. "Come, ladies, ze gentlemen should be ready for our return. It is time for ze women's ending ritual."

As the ladies stood, Olivia put aside her teacup with uncertain hands. She could not like the sound of the word "ritual." She slowly rose to her feet as well, only to have her hand taken up on either side by two of the ladies. The group, forced by the furniture, formed an oval, rather like some prayer circles of which Olivia had been a part, although they'd never held hands. Miss Lyons raised her face, assessing each woman in the circle before she spoke.

"Oh, Great Mother, we zank you for the gifts of your soil, and zank you also for imbuing zem with the healing properties of which you have so wisely given zem." She centered her attention on Olivia. Somehow her expression did not match her words; where she spoke humbly, her features seemed haughty, almost as if she were laughing under her reverent words.

"Now let us dance," she said.

Olivia startled as the woman next to her, Lady Lichfield, raised her voice in a chanting moan, the words either nonsense or in a tongue other than any of which Olivia knew. One by one the other ladies joined in, their voices blending with the simple melody as they began to step to their left, a long winding circle of dance with simple, forward-and-back footsteps.

Olivia was propelled along for a moment, but then the room's many scents made her head swim, and the chant disturbed her, and the dance struck her as a bit more pagan than she cared for it to be. She snatched her hands free, pressing them into the folds of her skirts so they might not be caught up again. This was too much, too bizarre. This...this rite might not be sacrilegious, but it felt perilously close. There was a point beyond which one's presence did not signify independence and courage, but rather giving in to pressure and participating in what was untrue to one's self.

The circling stopped, as did the moaning song, as the ladies turned as one to stare at Olivia.

"Is she not with us?" one lady asked.

"Apparently not," Miss Lyons said blandly, but there again was that not quite hidden smug smile.

"I--! These are not my ways," Olivia said. "You must pardon me. I must go home now." She turned and hurried to pull open the salon door--which she was a bit relieved to find unlocked. The last sight she had of the room was of Miss Lyons making soothing motions with her hands. But then Olivia was out of the room, sucking in fresher air, and hurrying away from the disturbing scene, beyond the reach of their voices.

She was almost running by the time she left the hallway and came into the dining room. The men were gathered in one corner, sitting with pipes and cheroots, and snifters balanced in their hands. They turned as one when she made her sudden appearance.

***

At the sight of a plainly distressed Lady Stratton, Ian sprang away from the fireplace where he'd placed one foot upon the fender, his snifter quickly discarded. Her face was pale, her comportment distraught. "Lady Stratton, is everything well?" he called as he walked swiftly to her side.

Lord Quinn came from his chair in Ian's wake, concern marking his features. "My lady?"

"My carriage. Please," she said to both men at once, her eyes darting between them. She licked her lips, took a breath, and made an effort at composing herself.

"What happened?" Lord Quinn asked.

124

"Why, merely a spot of spilled tea, I see," Lord Ewald said, stepping close to her and thrusting a kerchief into her hands. He helped her hands to rise, mimed with one hand that she ought to blot her gown, and half-turned to the group with a chagrined smile. "A spill is always so awkward. The lady chooses to remove to her home. You'll see her carriage is brought around, won't you, my good man?" he said to Quinn.

Olivia nodded, relief flooding her face as she belatedly patted her gown front with the kerchief, hiding the lack of any mark there.

"Of course," Lord Quinn replied stoutly, but his look remained troubled. "As it is your desire, I'll see your coach is readied at once, Lady Stratton."

Since one hand yet clutched Ian's kerchief to her bosom, Lord Quinn took up her free hand and escorted her from the room. Ian made to follow, but Quinn scowled at him and shut the dining room door in his face.

***

Immediately once they were in an entirely different--and quite normal looking--salon, Lord Quinn turned to her; Olivia had forgotten to maintain the illusion. "There is no stain," he said, but there was no accusation in his words. In fact, he looked remorseful. "Something has alarmed you," he said. "Me, the ladies, our way of thinking--"

She shook her head, but her mouth would not lie. "A little," she admitted.

He sighed. "My apologies, my lady. I realize-- I did warn you that something of this evening might seem unusual to you. But, come, 'unusual' does not necessarily mean 'unfortunate,' you must know. I pray you don't judge from so small a thing as convention."

"No," she murmured vaguely, looking away from his anxious expression. It was somehow more alarming to see his distress, for he was not a man to display such an emotion. All she knew was she wished to be rid of this place, and especially those ladies. "They...," she had to swallow, but then she went on, "they seemed to me to be like...like witches."

"Oh no," he said, then gave a small, exasperated laugh. "No, not witches. They are merely practicing ancient arts. Tell me, please, what did they do?"

"They drank strange teas. And...they danced. And sang this...this moany song..." Said aloud, it hardly sounded malevolent. She began to feel a bit foolish.

"I bid you, think twice," Lord Quinn said, taking up both her hands as he implored her with words and a steady gaze. "You wouldn't have thought a thing amiss had they stitched a quilt together, which you must admit is a very, very old art, now would you?"

"No. But... It was all so very strange. And... Oh dear, I know I sound a perfect ninny." She glanced up at him from under her lashes, regretting she'd allowed herself to make a scene.

"But I understand, my dear. You fear I will insist that all my guests must believe as I do. I could wish it were so, but, no, I am a realist." He gave a little laugh; it was meant to disarm, and she admitted it succeeded rather well. "I know people, my lady." His voice warmed, a persuasion. "I insist on nothing. I hope you know that you needn't feel you must believe as I do for us to remain...friends."

That word carried a wealth of meaning. She could not look at him, aware there were sounds outside the room, aware that Lord Quinn was awaiting her response. Everything about him, his voice and his stance, said that word was more than a mere offer of friendship on his part. She'd never before seen him ruffled, yet now he was. It was clear she'd risen into favor in his eyes, but that now he was fretting whether he was quite beyond the pale in her regard. As flattering as that was, it was also unsettling. He had to think he sensed a tolerance in her--and she was not so sure she felt it in herself, or if she wanted to.

"I will speak plainly, my lady. I see in you a like spirit," he confirmed. "One who can reason, and adapt, and grow." He took a breath, and went on. "With the All-Goddess's help, I wish to find a helpmeet, a mate of common heart. Oh, I know, I speak too soon! Please, do not tell me 'no' or 'stop.' Not until I have said all. Please know, you need not fear. I know these matters of the heart take time, and the Mother's blessings, if they are to come to be. Only say you will not avoid me. Only say you will allow me to continue as your friend. Let me prove myself to you, show you that I am a man of honor. That is all I ask, for now. Surely you can give me so little a thing as an evening or two? A smile? An agreement to not cast me off because I am just a little more willing than the average man to pursue the truth as I know it to be...?"

At last he ran out of words, standing, holding her hands, his eyes beseeching.

Just then the door to the hall opened, and Lord Ewald stood there, his eyes stormy. He'd clearly been seeking her.

"My lady's carriage is ready," said Quinn's butler from behind Lord Ewald. The man stood uncertainly, the lady's cloak and bonnet at hand.

The butler and Lord Ewald looked at them, the way Olivia and Lord Quinn stood so close, her hands caught up in his, how near to him she stood, and Ewald's mouth tightened.

"Should I offer my felicitations?" he ground out.

Tonight, Olivia had been annoyed with Ewald, thankful for his presence--and now she resented his tone. She pulled her hands free from Quinn's, dashed past both men who vexed her, snatched up her belongings, and fled out the front door.

"Proceed at once," she snapped at her driver, who swung her door closed behind her and climbed up to the box to at once to touch the whip to the horses.

She knew two male faces stared after her, but, thinking repeatedly the word *freedom*, she refused to turn back to glance at either one of them.

# Chapter 12

Olivia lived only a two-minute drive from the home of Lord Quinn. That was not nearly enough time to begin to clear her mind and sort through the many impressions that had assailed her tonight. She was, therefore, utterly unprepared to hear her name as her carriage door was pulled open.

"Lord Ewald!" she huffed, exasperated to see him there and to know he'd followed her carriage with his own.

"May we speak a moment?" He didn't wait for her answer, instead climbing into her carriage. He waved the driver back, and shut the door with a decided click. Olivia felt more than saw him turn toward her in the darkened interior.

"What happened at Quinn's to upset you?"

She sat up straighter. "I'm not obliged to tell you that. Although I thank you for assisting--"

"Tell me," he insisted. "Did anyone hurt you?"

She let out a breath, then chose to answer. "No. 'Tis merely I find much that occurs in that house...peculiar."

"Ah," he said, and she could make out enough of him to see he relaxed back into the squabs. He was silent for a long moment, peering back through the gloom even as she tried to do with him.

"I've known stranger men than Quinn, but it's a fact that he's unusual. Especially for a titled Englishman." He reached to open the coach door, letting in a little light that spilled from her house. He looked her up and down. "Too, you must be made aware the man is infatuated with you."

Growing vexed again, Olivia sat forward abruptly, giving her hand to the driver, who had moved near when the door reopened. "I believe that also," she said crisply, not looking at Lord Ewald as she descended from the carriage.

He followed her out. "And...?"

" 'And,' my lord?"

"And do you care to forward such a connection?"

Back stiff, she walked up her front stairs; here was a rusted knight, questioning the queen. "I cannot see where that is any of your affair, my lord."

To her surprise he gave a small laugh. "Well, that has put me in my place, has it not?" Having followed her, he rapped on the front door, correctly assuming it would be locked since night had fallen. "But I refuse to stay in my place without a word or two. My lady, I merely wished to be sure you're certain Quinn's ways are ones with which you really wish to associate."

She could pretend at ignorance--but there was no virtue in that. She'd decided to create a new life, not a dishonest one. "I do not see eye-to-eye with Lord Quinn on a number of matters," she admitted. "I find some of the things he does, the company he keeps...strange."

Ian nodded, but he surprised her by asking a question on a different topic. "My lady, will you tell me, on the night of the masquerade why did you use a French accent?"

Olivia tsked her tongue, but she answered. "I was afraid to let everyone know it was I under the mask." She ducked her chin, not wanting to see if he found her ridiculous. How could he not, since she'd been behaving that way?

"Why?"

She looked up from under her lashes. "I was breaking mourning early. And--" *Mercy, must I ever blush in front of this man?* "And I really wasn't sure of my welcome."

She saw his brows rise in surprise. "By the *haute ton*? A well-to-do, beautiful widow? How could you *not* be welcomed by society?"

Instead of blushing deeper yet, her displeasure faded and she almost laughed. "Goodness, we are so candid with each other, always," she said, shaking her head with a touch of amazement.

He smiled sideways, and she abruptly wished she'd not been a silly chit tonight. Then, abruptly, with something like a hard poke to the chest, she wished he'd bend down and kiss her, now, while there was light and while they could know whom they kissed. *Do* not *lean in toward him...*

To get past the shatteringly inappropriate fancy, she mumbled out a peculiar question of her own. "They...Quinn's practitioners, they wouldn't really *disrobe* together, would they?"

Did his grin expand? "I believe it's possible they might. May I assume this is not a practice to which you'd choose to subscribe?"

"Certainly not!" The shocked words came out just as her butler, Timmons, opened the door to them.

"Then may I be so bold as to suggest you sever your acquaintance with Lord Quinn?" Lord Ewald said.

Olivia turned on her own threshold, blocking the entry. She eyed him, no longer exactly angry but most assuredly done this night with challenging men. "I shall consider it, my lord. But any such choice will be my own. For now, I bid you good evening." She stepped back, and for the second time tonight a door was closed in Lord Ewald's face.

***

*She doesn't care for Quinn's ways,* Ian told himself as he rode home in his carriage. *She was frightened tonight. So, given those things, why wouldn't she just say she'd have no more to do with the man?*

By the time he'd returned to and strode into his home, he'd reached no conclusion as to the confusing nature of womankind.

He went to the library to find a brandy, over which he asked himself some serious questions about a subject that ought not concern him much. Still, the questions formed: what manner of woman was Lady Stratton? She seemed demur--but she accepted Quinn's company, the exact opposite of demur. She went where she liked, without chaperonage--but a widow was free to do so. And what about that gown she'd worn to the masquerade? It had exposed too much of her bosom, and her ankles had been on display. She'd pretended to be someone else. She'd kissed Ian in the mews, in the dark, hungrily, and all while not knowing a single thing about him, a complete stranger to her.

Well, it all added up to one thing, didn't it? She was not an appropriate sort. He would not court her. She would not be considered to become his wife.

Ian poured himself another brandy, aware he was angry at his own conclusion.

He might have drunk himself into his bed, except his butler came into the library.

"My lord, the man you spoke of?" Kellogg said. "A Frenchman? He is here. In the kitchens." The man sniffed with disapproval. "Eating everything within reach, I might add."

Ian put down his brandy, clapped Kellogg on both arms, and cried, "Well done, man." Then he hurried at once to see the elusive French informer for himself.

# Chapter 13

The next night, Olivia completed her nod in response to Miss Lyons's own, and carefully schooled her face not to reflect her dismay. Her brother had just invited the woman to join them in Alexander's theater box.

Olivia considered leaving the box to stroll, or claiming the megrims meant Alexander must take her home at once.

She refrained for a curious reason: this was Lord Quinn's hostess. If Olivia ignored Lord Ewald's unsolicited advice, and if she meant to retain Lord Quinn's company, she would of necessity come time and again into Miss Lyons's circle. Olivia wouldn't have minded giving Miss Lyons the cut direct based on the woman herself...but she thought, for now, she might just care to keep Lord Quinn's friendship.

His household had upset her, it was true. His fervent words had put her on her guard, she could not deny. And yet, when she'd closed her door on Lord Ewald last night and found her sleepless bed, her review of the strange night had condemned much...all but for Lord Quinn himself. He seemed so sincere in his convictions that she found it difficult to think of him as being sinister. He was very forthright, but thoughtful; he'd complied at once when she'd wished to have her carriage brought around. He'd tried to prepare her for strangeness. If she accepted him as he so openly was, was he at any kind of fault?

No. She decided that while Lord Quinn was unique, he was not diabolical. In fact, there was something...was sweet the correct word? about him.

However, she would be chary of stating the same for some of his guests...but then a man could not be blamed for the actions of others, and that was only the truth. So, she would do as he had asked, by remaining cordial with him, by refusing to react thoughtlessly to his atypical ideas. However, she mustn't flirt with him, as once she'd thought she might. She didn't want to imply her tolerance was more like acceptance. She must be polite, kind, forbearing...and gently rebuking when or if he went too far in any wise.

When it came to how to deal with Miss Lyons, that was another matter. Olivia couldn't erase from her mind's eye the look on the woman's face when Miss Lyons had given her invocation for the women; where Lord Quinn had appeared a man at prayer, Miss Lyons had looked like a siren setting a trap for an unknowing sailor. A clever, unkindly amused look had been on her face, and Olivia couldn't forget she'd seen it, no matter how guileless the lady might try to appear otherwise.

Alexander, to Olivia's relief, placed himself between her seat and that of Miss Lyons. Olivia leaned forward to the edge of the box, pretending to devote herself entirely to the performance, but had to give up the practice when both her brother and Miss Lyons continued to direct comments to her.

"You were quite well last night?" Miss Lyons asked her, a flash behind her eyes.

"Last night?" Alexander asked.

"Lord Quinn had a small gathering of friends for a midnight meal," Miss Lyons explained.

"Including you?" Alexander demanded of Olivia. His tone said he was both surprised and not approving.

"Yes."

134

"I cannot like your acquaintance with that man," Alexander said, twisting to Miss Lyons. "Pardon my frankness, m'dear, for I know you are his friend."

"Alexander, everything was well," Olivia lied.

"No offense taken," Miss Lyons said to Alexander. To Olivia, "I am glad to hear you found it all well. I zought perhaps you were taken ill. Or zat perhaps you had taken a distaste of ze company?"

Olivia gave the woman a quelling look. What was she playing at? And, really, it was a bit much that Alexander had concern etched upon his brow. Where had he been all those years when she'd really needed some brotherly support? She made no attempt to pacify Alexander and instead answered Miss Lyons with candor. "A distaste of Lord Quinn's company? Not at all. I shall be quite pleased to be his guest again. When and as I choose."

Alexander continued to frown. On his other side Miss Lyons, instead of seeming offended by the frosty tones, stretched out a hand in front of Alexander and patted Olivia's own where it rested in her lap. "Oh, I am so glad. Richard... Lord Quinn, he does so enjoy when ze ladies come to fill the evening. He was a bit cross with me last night. He seemed to zink I might have said or done something out of place." This last was said with a gentle little wrinkling between the lady's brows, as though she were puzzled at the very idea.

Olivia would have none of that. She'd let this woman know right here and now that such playacting would not be tolerated. "I always choose exactly when I will arrive and when I will leave. It's nothing to do with the present company whatsoever."

Miss Lyons's nostrils flared ever so delicately. Alexander looked bemused at Olivia, a fact she noted after a heartbeat, and therefore tried to give him a bit of a reassuring smile.

A slow, manufactured smile of her own spread over Miss Lyons's lips, and she gave a practiced little laugh. "But of course. How you relieve my mind, Lady Stratton," she said.

Alexander spread his frown between the two ladies, obviously perplexed. "I say, Olivia, I'd like to insist that I come along if you go to Lord Quinn's again--"

Both ladies spoke at once.

"Nonsense."

"You are most welcome," Miss Lyons's voice trailed after Olivia's.

The women eyed at each other.

"Well, I would," Alexander muttered, staring straight ahead as though he had suddenly decided the singer on stage was utterly compelling.

Some time passed before either lady spoke again, but then Miss Lyons shared a few desultory *on dits* with Alexander, and he visibly relaxed at the change in conversation.

"Tell me, Lord Hargood, do you know ze new gentleman who has come to town so recently? Lord Ewald?"

Olivia shifted in her chair.

"Yes, we've met. He's well-enough spoken of, although time will tell, eh? He's too new to the *ton* for whispers yet. Anyway, none seem to have followed him from abroad."

"And you, Lady Stratton?"

Olivia thought about ignoring the woman--*why is she stirring the pot?*--but it was too reasonable a question. Alexander would find it odd if she snapped at Miss Lyons over it.

"How do you find him?" the Frenchwoman persisted.

"I couldn't say. I have scarce made the gentleman's acquaintance."

"Oh, forgive my presumption," said Miss Lyons. "I have seen you together several times, and zen the other night my lord viscount, he asked to stay at our gathering. He said to make his place setting next to yours, and I made an assumption... Oh, I do beg your pardon. I see I was mistaken. I just zought..."

Olivia's eyes had narrowed, first at the hollow apology, and secondly because she became aware that Alexander was growing aggravated again.

"Perhaps we have some friends in common, other zan Lord Ewald?" Miss Lyons soothed.

"Perhaps." Olivia heard the chill in her own voice.

"Zere is one man I know. He is of slender build, with dark, long hair, and a nose zat is hooked," she said.

Olivia, relieved this description meant nothing to her, gave a little shrug. "I cannot think who I might know to match that description. Does this fellow not have a name?"

"He is no one particularly important. A fellow countryman of mine, an old friend. His name is Georges," Miss Lyons said, watching the other woman carefully.

***

Lady Stratton revealed nothing, no flicker, no flush, no sign she knew of such a person. Lisette frowned internally. The woman had not met Georges Douzain, had not been told his name, or had suddenly learned how to hide her feelings very well.

No, not the latter.

Perhaps she, Lisette, had overplayed her hand? She'd hoped to find out at least something when the other woman was caught agitated and perhaps off-guard. It hadn't worked, had actually failed utterly, perhaps disastrously, if Lady Stratton had any contacts she might report to...? Lisette had avoided having any whispers attached to her name so far, despite her lineage and accent, with Quinn as her finest shield. Had she just dented her own armor?

Or perhaps Lady Stratton really didn't know anything of the traitor Georges Douzain? Perhaps Lady Stratton was merely a decoy? Or a pawn?

"Ahhh," Lisette said slowly, another thought coming to her. Possibly she had not overplayed her hand, after all. Perhaps Lady

Stratton could be further used as an unknowing participant in this game of international hide-and-seek.

"If you meet such a man, you must give me his direction, as I would so enjoy his company once again. Ah, but I have a zought! If you were to meet Georges, Georges Douzain, then you must *not* tell him I am in London. Just acquire his direction, and then I might have the great, good fun of surprising him with a visit, *n'est-ce pas?*"

"The only French person I know is you, Miss Lyons," Lady Stratton said. She stood. "I wish to stroll," she said her to brother, her tone sharp.

Alexander obediently stood as well, and Lisette saw he aggravated his sister by supplying an arm for each lady. She watched that lady consider dismissing Lisette's company, but in the end Lady Stratton pressed her lips together and allowed Lord Hargood to escort them both from the box.

Lisette pondered that Lady Stratton hadn't bowed under her brother's suggestion that Lord Quinn's company might not be suitable. The very pretty lady had a stubborn streak. She'd also not seemed to know of Georges Douzain. Yes, Lisette was increasingly thinking the woman was not the enemy, but only the enemy's tool. It was time to charm, not to clash.

The threesome came across acquaintances, Hargood and Lisette chatting easily while Lady Stratton mostly looked on. Lastly they were approached by Mr. Turrell, whose mundane chatter about yesterday's midnight meal with Lord Quinn seemed to relieve Hargood's censure toward his sister. Lisette threw in a comment or two, and even managed to draw some commentary from Lady Stratton, who perhaps also preferred that her brother's concerns be assuaged. Thus Lisette began mending fences with her rival.

A less pinched-looking Lady Stratton looked up, only to now flush with color and lower her eyes once more. Lord Ewald was coming directly at her, smiling a greeting. *Ah ha! What is this?*

Lisette looked to Lady Stratton's stance and saw not so much rejection as fluster. This was not the posture of a woman who had "scarce made the gentleman's acquaintance," but a woman who was unsure how to behave before him. Rising red in her cheeks confirmed Lisette's speculation. *Could Lady Stratton prefer this man over Quinn?* And if so, could Ewald be used to keep the woman's eyes from Lisette's comfortable, convenient, and not-to-be-lost sponsor?

Lisette put on a smile and called a honeyed greeting as Lord Ewald approached.

***

Ian saw Lady Stratton's gaze center on him, and saw her face redden, but he didn't know how to interpret the response. She'd been aggravated with him when they'd parted last night; was he to have a cool reception?

As he stopped before her party, she offered him a little curtsy and a nod of the head--but more importantly, a direct look, which he welcomed. It seemed he was not to be whipped for yesterday's sins.

That was all to the good--but what startled him was a sudden lack of poise on his part, an unanticipated thudding in his chest, when she further relented and gave him a tiny greeting smile.

He'd lain awake until near dawn, recalling their parting words. And then on to every word, every gesture the lady had ever made in his presence, both as the Cat and as Lady Stratton. He'd convinced himself he must have nothing more to do with her, not beyond mere politeness. He had a new life to shape, and she wasn't the one to help him form it.

Yet when, mimicking Miss Lyons, she offered her hand, he bowed over it and saluted it with an airy kiss. Only to become aware his thumping heart now crawled up into his throat, blocking thought and breath for several beats, and he wanted nothing so much as to impossibly keep on holding her hand.

*What is wrong with you, you nodcock? Yes, she's pretty enough...more than pretty. And she's charmingly dressed, the feathers in her hair curling near her ear and whispering "touch me, touch me..." And I wonder if she knows her mouth is poised as if for kissing? And her smile is so warm, so...* Ian swallowed hard and gave the tiniest shake of his shoulders, rallying his thoughts.

"My lady," he said, letting her hand go at last.

Perhaps she'd taken the little shiver as some form of rejection, for her smile faltered. The pounding in his chest became a stab, one that went straight through him, actually painful. He longed to explain himself, except what could he possibly say?

*Why this school-boy idiocy? You're years past such instant, ridiculous infatuation, you fool...*

"Ewald," Hargood said, and the two men exchanged bows, Ian's perhaps a touch shaky. Hargood looked from his sister to Ian. "I understand you've already met my sister?"

"I've had that privilege."

"And you've clearly met Miss Lyons."

"Indeed."

"We were just growing weary of strolling," the latter said. "Why do you not join us in our box, Lord Ewald?"

He looked to Olivia, half-expecting to see denial in her features, but she gave a nod and pulled up another smile. It was more than encouragement to him. *Ridiculousness, foolishness, folly.* He meant to say no, but heard himself say, "Thank you, I will."

They moved into the box just as the curtain was opening for the second act, Hargood on Miss Lyons's right, and Ian seated between the two ladies. They shared some desultory conversation between the moments of action onstage. Good. This was good. He was behaving normally. This was all he wanted in her company. He would maintain discipline over his involuntary responses to the lady's charms, and her smile, and her... Ian sat up straight and applied his attention to the actor on stage.

At the play's end, Ian ignored his own counsel that he ought bid them good evening, instead keeping the threesome's company as they moved from the theater. *Really, one must be polite.* Miss Lyons was on Hargood's arm, and Lady Stratton walked beside Ian, keeping a not undue measure of space between them.

He was surprised when she slowed her steps, letting her brother get a little ahead. She seemed to have to make a little effort to meet his gaze. "My lord, I never thanked you for assisting me last night. You saw my distress, and you moved to aid me."

He gave a brief nod. "Of course."

"Not 'of course.' Not every man chooses to be gallant. I thank you."

The light evening breeze again teased the three egret feathers that curled over the top of her head to nearly tickle her ear, and gave him something to gaze at other than her mouth.

"You're welcome. My lady, will you drive with me tomorrow afternoon?" It was the side of his brain that wanted to re-explore her lips that asked the question.

Her voice was small, but he felt truly relieved--and exasperated with his relief--when she said, "Yes."

"Come along, Olivia," called Hargood, looking over his shoulder as he handed Miss Lyons up into his coach.

"Good evening then, Lady Stratton. Until tomorrow. At two?"

"Yes. Good evening." She looked into his face, and for a moment it seemed she might say something more, but then her lips came together so that one corner of her mouth rose in a half-smile, a personal smile, a friend's smile, and there was a new, not wholly unpleasant ache in the area of his sternum while she dipped him a curtsy.

She turned and allowed Hargood to hand her up, settling onto the squabs opposite Miss Lyons, while her brother settled at the other lady's side. As their carriage rolled away, Ian waited for his own.

All the while, he named himself a great, indecisive fool--one who calculated he had best use all fifteen hours until he saw her again to buttress his too-easily-crumbled resolutions.

***

In the late evening hours, Georges looked up from his seat on a slim bed in a fourth-story bedroom in Lord Ewald's home; the viscount had returned from the theater and had come up to quietly knock on his door.

"*Monsieur*," Ewald greeted him as he closed the door behind himself. He looked around, clearly discovering the simple room held no chair. After Georges had stood and bowed to him, Ewald had waved him to be seated again and had remained standing himself, folding his hands together before him.

"I have yet to receive the instructions from Sir Terrence." Georges grunted at the information. "You are well? Do you require anything?"

Georges could not much complain. The room was ever a little cold, but his meals were faithfully supplied, the linens were clean, and Ewald had provided a handful of books in French from his library. Georges had been given wine from the cellars to drink. He was a little drunk now, in fact, because besides the room being cold his one complaint was boredom, and the wine helped a little with both.

"I am well, zank you, my lord," Georges murmured. As agreed, he'd secluded himself in the small room, with meals brought by but one footman, and his chamberpot carried away by the same; the idea was to allow the other servants to forget he hid among them. It was good advice, as both he and the viscount waited for Sir Terrence's notice that a ship with a reliable captain was ready to receive Georges and bear him away to greater safety.

"Your evening was pleasant?" Georges asked, making an effort to be a cordial, if confined, guest.

"Yes, quite," Ewald said. "The play was well, and Madame Catalani sang. She's remarkable." He was clearly making conversation. Georges appreciated the man for trying to relieve in at least a small way the tedium of waiting, to say nothing of providing this temporary sanctuary. "Lady Stratton and Miss Lyons were quite taken with her voice."

Georges stopped breathing as Ewald chatted about other performers. *Miss Lyon? Lisette Lyons!* The very woman he'd seen at Lord Quinn's masquerade. *She keeps company with Ewald?*

He only half-listened as Ewald went on to give him some news of the day, instead pondering with narrowed eyes why Ewald would tell him about Lisette Lyons?

He wouldn't, not if the man was her confederate.

No, and so Lord Ewald couldn't know he held a viper to his breast. A viper which might not strike at the Englishman but would certainly strike out at Georges if she got any hint where he was sheltered.

When Ewald left his side, Georges went down to his knees, reaching under the short-legged servant's bed to retrieve his traveling bag.

# Chapter 14

Under heavy gray clouds, Ian drove his curricle before her home, where he saw Lady Stratton--*Olivia*--through the windows of her front salon. Her head was bent, probably at some bit of stitchery, her golden-flame hair piled high. She looked up as the sound of his wheels rattled to a stop, and when she rose he caught a glimpse of a golden gown that took its cue from her hair color.

He tossed the leadstrings to the boy who came from the mews, and descended. Ian walked up the steps that led to her front door, and knocked. Her butler opened the door, gave him a bow, accepted Ian's shake of head denying a surrender of his three-caped coat, and escorted Ian into the large, airy chamber that served as Olivia's salon.

She came from a small room off to the left, obviously used as a cloakroom. Her gown was now hidden by a fur-lined soft gray pelisse, and she wore the new and fashionable Prussian helmet cap, black, ornamented with silver tassels. Her gloved hands carried a fur muff against the November chill. She looked utterly appealing, and her smile was welcoming. He had to fight to keep his own smile impartial.

"My lady. You're prepared."

"Prepared for cold." She glanced out the window. "And rain? I cannot like the dark edges on the clouds."

"Only the heartiest of souls will be out," he agreed. "Happily, my curricle boasts a hood should rain come."

"Then let us go see who is as mad as we," she agreed, taking his offered arm and making him smile despite himself.

Hyde Park was dismal in its late autumn grays and browns, but they found they were not utterly alone in taking advantage of a less crowded park. As Ian drove his curricle, they met the Duke of Dorset on his white horse, and a younger set stopped to chat for several minutes, but mostly it was a simple drive where they didn't halt much, merely nodding to acquaintances as they passed.

The fashionable hour came and went, and still they lingered, circling the park again. Ian had thought to bring rugs, which they pulled up from folds around their feet, against the cold.

It was not until the setting sun was particularly direct in his vision that Ian realized how much time had gone by. *Her company is an easy, comfortable thing,* he noted with a sigh.

Although they'd avoided rainfall, the cold had made her nose turn pink, and she'd long since tucked her gloved hands inside the muff. "You are feeling the cold," he said.

"I am," she admitted. "I see why near-winter rides are not usually all the rage."

"My apologies."

"Oh, not at all! I am glad for it." She looked away. "I have spent far too much time tucked away inside my house." He heard the wistfulness in her voice. Here he was looking for a home and wife, . and she was looking to be free of her house and her mourning.

He was not wholly easy with his turn of thought, and randomly changed the subject. "I say, Miss Lyons was quite pleasant last night. I'd had the feeling the two of you were not bosom beaux, but she didn't seem to know it. Or am I all the way mistaken?"

Olivia did not try to hide how her mouth tightened, although her expression lightened in a moment. "I'll not say a word," was her tartly humored response, but instantly made a lie when she said, "Though I do find she says the oddest things."

146

"Such as . . . ?"

"Such as asking if we share common acquaintances."

"That's a very old diversion. How is it you object?"

"Oh, it's not the asking that disturbs me. But why she would insist I must tell her the direction of a gentleman I have never met? Is this something the French do? Some sport of theirs?"

Ian checked his horses, slowing their progress a little, his old habits making him at once note that something was out of place. He scowled. "No. I think not. What sort of man does she ask after?"

"I don't know," Olivia said with a dismissive motion of her hand. "A Frenchman. With a hooked nose. Georges...something? I am unsure if that is a Christian or surname."

His hands tightened on the reins, accidentally causing his horses to come to a halt. He rattled the strings and clucked to them to get them moving again, and cleared his throat as he thought.

"If anyone would know such a Frenchman," she went on, "surely it would be she? Or is she somehow trying to boast of an acquaintance? Well, I am an inadequate person for that game, if so. I know scarce enough of society to be impressed."

It was too much of a coincidence. What connection did *Mademoiselle* Lyons have with Douzain? Why would she be asking after him?

Perhaps Miss Lyons was only what she seemed: a displaced aristocrat trying to make her way in an unsettled world--yet it was not in Ian's training to accept the apparent facts, but rather to garner for himself the particulars of any situation. He could not dismiss this flagrant incongruence as coincidence unless proved otherwise.

"You have gone quite silent," Olivia said at his side.

He glanced up and realized his horses were again scarcely moving because the leathers had gone lax, and that the sun was invisible behind the houses, only a thin yellow haze of twilight showing it had not completely disappeared yet. He called to the horses, rearranging the strings in his hands to make sure he got a bit more speed out of them.

"My apologies," he said to Olivia. "We've been out too long. I didn't mean to freeze you half to death."

She shook her head, unconcerned. "We will amuse my neighbors when they see I have the predicament of being frozen to my seat."

Her house was just ahead, so it was only half a minute later when he pulled up on the reins, bringing the horses to a halt. He half-turned to her. His eyes moved over her face, noting the soft smile playing around her mouth, the frank gaze she returned to his own. "You're in no danger of being in a predicament with me, my lady."

"None at all?" she asked with a pretend sulk and a stage sigh.

His breathing stopped for a moment, as if the gloaming that gathered around them had somehow entered his lungs and paralyzed them. She was merely making a small joke, he knew it, but there was a part of him that refused to understand, that wanted to take her words as a gentle rebuke. There was nothing a gentleman could do, after all, if he were rebuked except to offer an apology. And his apology seemed to want to take only one form, that of a kiss. Perhaps it was the playful pout of her lips. Or maybe it was that one minute of magic, which floats in the twilight just before the day is done and the night fallen, that made him lean forward and press his mouth ever so lightly to her own.

She jumped a little, but after a long moment she leaned into him, accepting his kiss.

When they parted, scarce a heartbeat later, he didn't reach for her hand, as every instinct told him to, and he didn't lean further into her in return, as his body screamed at him to do. Instead he just sat very close, his mouth two inches from hers, trying to understand why he'd done it when he knew he shouldn't. It wasn't fair to play with her, a woman who could easily find another man to suit her. *A man like Quinn…?*

"Take yer leads there, m'lord?" a voice interrupted.

Ian wheeled away from Olivia, seeing a groom standing gazing up at them uncertainly. Tossing the strings down to the lad, Ian leaped to the ground with an alacrity the lady might find unflattering, the skin of his face blazing scarlet as it hadn't done in years. He came around, offering a hand to Olivia, who hesitated then placed the very ends of her fingers on his hand as she descended.

He understood her reticence. She'd been merely teasing, and he'd not responded in kind. Add to that, there was no social contrivance for acknowledging intimacies of connection that had come far before their usual time; what did it say that she always accepted his kisses, especially when any true, ordinary, *real* courtship wouldn't have included them so soon?

What did it say that he continued to flout his own advice and to take kisses from her?

Ian climbed back onto the curricle, receiving the strings from the groom. He paused a long time, letting the dusk's wind soothe his reddened face as he watched as the one-time Lady Cat made her way inside.

*Attraction. Wife. Home. Suitability.* The words seemed to clash.

He sat a long time, until the groom asked again if he required anything. As he absently shook his head in response, Ian found the idea that had been eluding him, that had made him stay and stare at the Widow Stratton's house: what made a home? He, who had so often moved from abode to abode, country to country, was one man who absolutely knew that a home was not made from things or bits of land, but from people.

Further, he was utterly certain one person could make a little piece of the world completely un-foreign. He knew true sanctuary could be, *was*, found not in the space of a nation, or a house, or even a room, but in the touch of a loved one's arms.

But...was there a right kind of love? Or, conversely, a love that might grow and pull and demand, but in the end fit all wrong?

He took a deep breath, set the horses to their paces, guiding them not toward his home, but toward Westminster. He knew to whom in the foreign office it would be most auspicious to speak, to finally bring the matter of the French informant--and a possible Frenchwoman spy--to a close. For close it he would, so that the rest of his life could begin.

# Chapter 15

Two nights later, Olivia tried to hide behind her sister. Lord Ewald had just been announced and was casting his gaze about the room. She shouldn't have come with Phoebe to Lady Mackleby's ball, but she'd thought it might serve as a diversion to her muddled, tumbling thoughts--thoughts of the very man from whom she hid.

Phoebe gave her younger sister a speaking glance, and followed it with a rather caustic observation. "What is this missishness of a sudden?"

"I'm tired. That last dance..." Olivia mumbled.

Phoebe clicked her tongue. "Now, Olivia, what are you about these days?"

"Me?"

"Yes, you. One week you're never to be seen, the next you're at every ball and rout in London, and keeping company with London's most talked-about people. Now you're wilting like a frightened schoolgirl." When Olivia didn't answer, merely taking on a disgruntled look, Phoebe went on. "Look at yourself. You're dashing! You've been dressing in every vibrant color of the rainbow. This rich blue silk is quite fine on you, I must say. Did you order the gloves with matching embroidery, or did you find them in a shop?"

"Sampson's Warehouse," Olivia muttered.

Phoebe rallied from her temporary distraction. "Never mind that. You smile, you dance, you flirt--or at least you did until ten minutes ago. What am I to think, with such rapid changes in your mood? And if your own sister cannot fathom what you are about, then you can only imagine what the tattlemongers will have to say."

"I don't lend an ear to gossip, and neither should you," Olivia snapped.

"And what of these men you dance with? Mr. Turrell? Mr. Newlin? Captain Russell? Lord Quinn? Some of them are rackety fellows at best, my girl, and I have to think you know it."

"But it's merely a dance shared, Phoebe," Olivia said in some exasperation. She couldn't like this newfound habit of her siblings attempting to oversee her social life. *Where were you when I had none?*

"I hear it is more than that. I hear you were at a late meal at Lord Quinn's house, and came home even later. And you had strong words with Lord Ewald on your doorstep. See there, you do not deny it."

*Neighbors and their chatter!* "Oh, Phoebe. How you do go on. I'm no longer a child, and none of that is truly shocking." She was not about to say that it had, in fact, been rather shocking to her as the evening had worn on, for that would just be more grist for Phoebe's mill.

But Phoebe's scold had altered, shifting into a sharper interest. "So tell me, what did you and Lord Ewald squabble over?"

"If you must know, he interfered in my life, as you do now. He bid me not to see Lord Quinn anymore." Olivia looked down her nose at her sister, daring her to agree with the man.

Phoebe's reply was never to be known, because the object of their discussion, Lord Quinn, stepped before them. He looked well in buff pantaloons and a blue coat to match his dark blue eyes.

He bowed. "Ladies. I pray the evening finds you well," he spoke to them both, but his eyes were all for Olivia.

"It does," Olivia answered. "My lord, I believe you already know my sister, Mrs. Tilman?"

"I've had that privilege." He gave a quick greeting smile to Phoebe, only to immediately return his regard to the younger sister. "I was hoping you were free for the next dance and would be willing to bestow it upon me."

Olivia felt Phoebe stiffen beside her and became aware of the perfect way to distinctly inform her sister she must mind her own business: she offered her hand to Lord Quinn at once. "That would be all that is delightful."

Phoebe made an uncertain noise, but Olivia was escorted to the edge of the dance floor and chose not to give it any more thought. She felt a flash of pleasure at her act of independence.

It was only then, as she chatted inconsequentially with Lord Quinn as they waited for the music to begin, that she recalled she'd been attempting to hide from Lord Ewald. The sudden realization caused her to circle the ring of waiting couples with her eyes; she found Lord Ewald across the way, off the dance floor, standing alone. He was lounging against a support column, his arms casually crossed in front of his silver-worked waistcoat, his black evening clothes fitting him so well as to make his tailor's reputation. His eyes were on her, and as soon as she saw him, he made a bow in her direction. She hesitated a moment, chagrined to have put herself in the position of having to respond, and then gave a curtsy in return, to which he responded by inclining his head. She looked away at once, so as not to have to acknowledge the fact that the movement plainly said he'd seek her out later.

Lord Quinn followed the interchange, and perhaps because of it, when they squared off for the dance, her back had been placed to the other gentleman.

"Are you feeling well?" Lord Quinn ventured when half the dance was gone and she hadn't said more than a word or two, despite his fleeting attempts at conversation between movements.

"I'm quite well," she said, blushing a little. She was behaving quite unforgivably. Because one gentleman flustered her, she was neglecting the other. That would never do. In fact, if she was really in command of her life as she wished her siblings to believe her to be, she ought to be able to at least carry on a conversation despite her own inner inclination to sit down and think her confusion all the way through. It was not Lord Quinn's fault she felt increasing awkwardness in Lord Ewald's company.

That thought almost made her laugh, for any other lady would find just the opposite to be true, that it was Lord Quinn who ought to discomfort her and not the thoroughly non-Druid and genial Lord Ewald. But that was her very problem, of course. He was genial, likable, and overall had only treated her well, more of a friend than one had a right to expect on such short acquaintance.

That acquaintanceship could have gone on, would have been fine...if only he would cease kissing her...

*But...his last kiss had been so different somehow.* It had been so light, scarcely touching her mouth, barely there for even the length of a heartbeat. Yet still it had been brushed with attraction, and had awoken something that felt too much like appetite. She finally understood the elemental magnetism between a man and a woman, so sharp and clear and tempting that even the once reclusive Olivia felt it, tasted it, wanted to explore more of it. *All that, in the merest touch, for the merest stretch of time? Oh yes.*

It had also had the hint of a promise in it--until he'd pulled away, and the spell had broken.

She hadn't truly known she was wrong to encourage him, not until his pulling away showed her that even the briefest of caresses could connect you to a pull that was ruthless, making you want to fall into it with abandon; it was an especially cruel connection when, once made, it became severed.

Was it worse, knowing *why* he'd pulled away? For she'd grasped the cause at once: what man could want more of her, she who, out in those mews, had shown herself to him as a wanton? He distanced himself because he didn't want her, not in any respectable kind of way.

Perhaps not even disrespectable. He found her to be a low creature--and she could only admit her own actions had proved his point.

And now she was not only avoiding him, but neglecting Lord Quinn. Face burning, she nonetheless forced herself to suppress the heavy feelings of self-censure, for now. There would be time enough later, alone in her bed, for mental lashings.

She tried once, and then again, finally conjuring up a smile for Lord Quinn's benefit.

He responded to her smile. More than responded, for soon Lord Quinn was flirting with her quite openly. *You flirt with any man who will respond to you. How does that* not *make you seem a tart?*

When the dance ended and she made her curtsy, Lord Quinn must have seen she meant to take flight, because he caught her arm to prevent her leaving his side.

"If you might indulge me for a moment longer?"

Her mute nod was accepted at once.

"I speak bluntly at times, Lady Stratton," She nodded again, just wanting him to say his piece and let her leave. "And now I wish to tell you, directly, how pleased I am you do not shun my company."

"My lord--"

"I know you were shocked at my party. Yet, tonight you do not flee my presence just because, through me, you were exposed to new notions."

"I hope to be accepting of--"

"And I have been hoping, too, dear lady. Hoping for, waiting for, such a woman. An intelligent, thinking, rational woman." He stared down at her, a glow in his eyes. "Now that I've met you, I have to let you know I cherish your company." He took her hand and squeezed it possessively.

"My lord--!" she began.

She got no more words out, for Lord Quinn pulled her into his arms and kissed her. He was so much taller that she was held almost suspended in his arms, so it took her a moment to wriggle free of his embrace. "My lord!" she said again, scandalized.

If he was embarrassed to kiss a woman in public, and at a party not even his own, he gave no sign of it. "I know I shock you, my lady, but I wanted you to know. I want everyone to know of my regard for you."

"You ought to have at least warned me," she said, instead of the more obvious scold that he had no right to manhandle her thusly.

That was when she looked past him and saw Lord Ewald, frozen in place with a scowl, not twenty feet away.

*Now what must you think of me?* Nothing fine, she was sure. She gathered her poise and wrenched her eyes back to Lord Quinn. "Might I have a glass of lemonade?" she said in a voice she hoped was not as brittle as it sounded to her.

"Of course. I will fetch it for you at once," Lord Quinn said, tucking his arm to his waist for a little bow of acknowledgement. He hesitated a moment, as though he could not bear to part from her for even a minute, but then he stepped away.

The moment he left her side Olivia closed her eyes, filled with aggravation. Not only had she been involved in a scene that must surely cement Lord Ewald's opinion of her scandalous nature, but too, she'd overcorrected her error and allowed Lord Quinn to be encouraged. Perhaps Phoebe and Alexander were right to be looking over her shoulder; it seemed she was incapable of handling herself with any refinement.

Well, there was nothing for it. She must correct, again, her errors. She knew the surest way to change Lord Quinn's current assumption, and that was to simply abandon him, to see him no more.

A last glance toward Lord Ewald showed her he'd not moved so little as an inch toward her, and his eyes were yet rounded with something she feared was aversion.

She pushed her way into the crowd, her head hanging.

***

Lady Stratton didn't see Quinn turn back to her, two glasses in hand, nor the dismay on his face when he'd clearly lost sight of her in the crowd. Ian watched as Quinn put the glasses aside and pawed his way through people, head twisting from side to side to locate her direction.

Another man might have pointed him in Olivia's trail, but Ian had no such thought. Instead, his rather furiously spinning thoughts led him to wonder what it meant that she'd fled immediately after that outrageous and so-public kiss. She *was* fleeing, wasn't she? If she meant to rendezvous with Quinn, both of them were displaying peculiar behavior.

Unlike Quinn, Ian hadn't lost Olivia in the crowd. Thoughts still whirring, yet his body won over reason, and he moved swiftly after the retreating glimpses of blue silk.

She was gone through the door, and he hurried out into the night, faster and faster, to get her back in sight. He was rewarded for his lightness of foot when he saw her turn away from ordering her carriage be brought around.

He stepped rapidly to her side, where she waited just inside the reach of the lamp's glow outside Lady Mackleby's door. Perhaps he'd meant to scold her for the vulgarity of that unprivate kiss, but something in the way her eyes flashed and her lips thinned as he approached softened his rebuke.

Instead he merely asked, "You're leaving?"

She stepped back, to be out of his reach. "I am."

He stood without moving, undecided on what she was thinking or how to act himself.

He settled on a nobler course. "Do you require an escort?"

She didn't snap at him, or blubber, or act as if she didn't know he'd scowled at her for her kiss with Quinn. Indeed, she looked at him straight on, with more than a bit of challenge in the set of her chin. It crossed his mind that this was one of the reasons he was drawn to her: she had a tendency to meet things clear-eyed.

"My lord, let us be plain-spoken," she said, proving his thought. Her voice was crisp, but not exactly angry. She put back her head, looking up at him frankly. "Lord Quinn kissed me. I did not seek his kiss, nor did I kiss him in return. You, on the other hand, I did kiss back, and on purpose. That night, and since." Her face reddened, but she didn't drop her stare. "I confess, I let myself be forward with you, and inappropriate, and..." Now she blinked, seemingly not liking to say such things aloud. "And I quite understand that I acted beyond the pale. I am, in your eyes, not the sort of woman to be...serious about. But, sir, neither am I a wanton. I acted out of folly--and have learned the lesson it teaches. I shall not behave so again. Still, a first impression cannot be undone, I know that. I know you cannot admire me."

He stared down at her, aware his lips were parted to interrupt her.

But she went on. "We obliged each other with kisses, but no more. Such foolishness is behind us. There," she stated with a firm nod of the head. "Now we can start over. We can become friends, and that's all. If you like. Or not. I will completely accept your decision as to the matter."

She'd made him feel abashed with a few sentences. It didn't matter she hadn't said anything he hadn't thought--but the words sounded so judgmental, so how he'd shaped his thoughts but so against feelings that kept overtaking his intentions.

And...never to kiss her again...?

"It grieves me to hear I have given you such a harsh assessment of my sensibilities." *Sensibilities I regret, not least because I must have let her see them, and I couldn't wish to hurt her. I ache to see her poise, her grace in the face of censure; I've met soldiers who could not face judgment so squarely.*

He stepped toward her and returned a hand to her elbow, which at least she allowed. "I must take the blame for--"

A hand came down hard on his shoulder, spinning him around. Quinn stood there, towering over the two of them. He was visibly angry, his brows drawn together as though to echo the stiff line of his mouth. "My lord, I must ask you to leave off touching the lady," he said in a dark tone to Ian. His words were unnecessary since he'd already compelled Ian's touch to drop away, but the message of possessiveness was clear.

"Lord Quinn, everything is--"

Quinn spun on Olivia, calling out sharply, "Has he made you an offer?"

"No," she answered, going a bit pale.

He swung his heavy gaze back to Ian. "You are not *affianced* to the lady. You will therefore forbear from touching her henceforth."

Ian was shorter and lighter than Quinn, but he was not afraid to show umbrage as he pulled himself up to his full height. "And you speak for the lady, why?"

Lady Stratton's carriage arrived, the driver climbing down and eyeing the obviously tense gathering, looking for his clue on how to proceed.

"I speak for myself," Olivia said, nodding sharply at the driver, who scrambled to pull open the coach door and lower the steps.

"It's well enough, Olivia. I will go," Ian said, deliberately using her Christian name. He backed away from Quinn to make her a bow. "But I will call upon you in the morning." He did not make it an option, but a statement for Quinn to hear.

The big man's hands were balled into fists at his sides, and his face was flushed dark. "If he comes, you'll not receive him," he told Olivia.

Her shoulders went rigid. "I'll do as I decide to do." She stepped past the two men, quickly climbing in the coach, not looking at either as she pulled the door to with a slam.

Ian moved away, to where his not yet rigged chariot waited for his horse to be brought around, not caring for a round of fisticuffs with Quinn, like schoolboys in the street. Years as an agent had taught him it was often better to withdraw rather than inflame. If that was feeble, he was nonetheless perfectly content to see Lord Quinn spin and retreat back into the party.

\*\*\*

Lisette saw Lord Hargood return from outside, smelling of cheroot smoke, his back clearly up.

"What do you know of this Quinn fellow?" he demanded as he walked up to her.

"Lord Quinn?" She looked around with attention, locating Quinn in the crowd.

"Yes. Lisette, I know you like to act his hostess and all, but you have to admit the fellow's capable of raising a whisper or two. I think he might even be a scoundrel. And I just overheard him all but proposing to my sister. He and Ewald almost came to blows over it."

Lisette had reached out to lay a hand on Hargood's sleeve, and at his words her fingers tightened on the cloth like talons. She searched Quinn's darkened face across the room, his tight jaw, the

160

way he seemed to be preoccupied as he listened to one of the other guests.

"What was your sister's answer?" she asked, sure her expression had gone pinched.

Hargood shrugged. "Don't think it actually came to his asking. But she ran away, red-faced and agitated."

Lisette slowly uncurled her fingers from his arm, and pulled composure about her shoulders. "If it came to it, you do not wish her to marry Quinn?"

Hargood's scowl deepened, but he stopped short of pronouncing no. Lisette took that as an answer all the same, especially as it aligned with her own needs. "We must see to it zat no marriage goes forward," she announced firmly. She eyed Lord Hargood. "You will help me arrange an estrangement between zem."

Lord Hargood lowered his chin to his chest, but once again he failed to say no.

# Chapter 16

"Are you available to receive Sir Terrence, my lord?" Kellogg asked from the dining room doorway the next morning.

Ian looked up from his breakfast and nodded at once. He wiped his mouth with his napkin as Kellogg informed him, "Sir Terrence is in the morning room, my lord."

Ian closed the door behind him as he entered, and the two men exchanged bows and greetings. Sir Terrence crossed to him, handing him a sealed letter. "That tells you all you need to know about where to deliver our friend."

It only took a few moments to peruse the information: a time after dark tomorrow night, the name of a ship, her dock, and documents supplying a new identity for Douzain.

"Do you care to meet 'our friend'?" Ian offered.

Sir Terrence shook his head. "Less known, best managed."

They chatted for a few moments then, with thanks from one to the other, Sir Terrence bowed himself out. When he was gone, Ian removed the identity documents Douzain would need in his new life, put them in his coat pocket until he could stash them in the hidden and locked drawer in his library desk, but the information on time and tide, committed to memory, was in short order poked and stirred into nothing but tiny black flakes on the morning fire.

At last, Georges Douzain would be leaving London, and Ian would be an agent of the government no more.

He moved discreetly upward to the attics, timing his movements to avoid his own servants, not because he was suspicious of them but out of prudence, an old habit. Gossip was harder to come by if all seemed unchanged and unremarked.

Unfortunately, change *had* come: *Monsieur* Douzain, with his few possessions, had fled.

\*\*\*

Not an hour later, Olivia watched Lord Ewald--*Ian*--as he rode away. He'd come to call, as he'd said he would last night. Her heart was a leaden weight in her breast, which sank just a little lower as she saw he'd been made to ride away through rain and wind, without a chance of warming himself at her fire or partaking of her brandy, because she'd ordered her servants to say she wasn't at home to anyone, especially Lord Ewald.

It had cost her nothing to have Miss Lyons turned away when she'd come earlier, but refusing Ewald, despite all, made her throat thick with unshed tears. Plus part of her longed to know why he'd come; she'd given him his chance to abstain from her company. *Perhaps he doesn't think me completely unsuitable? Or...perhaps he came to be sure our conversation was finished, his disconnect made clear?*

She saw his horse stop in the street, long enough for him to look back at the house. She retreated from the window, but not before it was possible he'd seen her standing there.

Well, being caught in hoydenish behavior, gawping after him, must be the last straw; he could surely find no elegance or deportment in her behavior. She turned from the window, blinking back tears.

\*\*\*

Ian saw Olivia at her window. She'd drawn back at once, but he was sure it had been her.

Others might find him odd, but despite being turned away and having no chance to say his piece, his heart rallied; she'd cared enough to look out after him.

*My heart?* he asked himself as he resettled in his saddle. The rain and wind worked to be sure no part of him remained dry or comfortable, but despite it all he grinned. *Yes, my heart. It pounds, and flips, and sings, all to tell me the lady is undeniably special. To me.*

Although he'd had no chance to ask her, suddenly he thought she must not have accepted Lord Quinn. Had she, she would've admitted Ian and told him as much.

His smile widened, no doubt making him look a fool.

He drew a rather shaky breath, letting it out slowly.

Oh, well, yes, it was probably too soon to call this spinning, vexing, energizing elation as grand a thing as love…but he didn't care. Love could grow and expand--but it also had to start somewhere. And, ridiculously, a sad-faced woman staring out her window as she'd him sent away, encouraged him nearly as much as being admitted would have done. *And there's an end to my indecision. By Jove, I'm glad to be done with being an idiot.*

He urged his horse to a faster pace. The sooner he got home, the sooner he might learn what the Home Office operatives had learned of Georges Douzain's present location. Once he was found and set upon the ship, then, at long last, Ian would be rid of obligation or concern for anyone but the thoroughly irresistible Lady Stratton.

# Chapter 17

Not two hours later, Miss Lyons had returned to Olivia's doorstep. Only this time she'd not accepted "no" as an answer from the butler, and had quite literally pushed her way into Olivia's home.

Even worse, she'd brought a party with her, some dozen people Olivia scarcely recognized let alone welcomed, the two exceptions being Alexander and Lord Quinn. They'd all settled in, ordered food and drink and playing cards, and Olivia had pacified an outraged Mary Kate by saying she'd changed her mind and the guests were free to stay. Anyway, how was her butler and one footman to expel a dozen people, for pity's sake, not least her own brother?

The sun had gone down nearly an hour ago; they'd stayed all day, and Olivia wished she'd listened to her maid after all. The only thing that kept her from rising and stating they must leave was that she knew Lord Quinn wouldn't go with them. His gaze had been almost constantly on her since he'd arrived. She just knew he'd stay behind, and she'd be forced to try to either have the powerful Quinn physically removed by her meager staff, or else she'd have to entertain his attentions alone. She didn't care to do either, particularly the latter.

It was a gay gathering, she had to admit that, regardless of her own tedium. Everyone else was laughing and enjoying themselves. Had it been two days earlier, she had no doubt she'd have found the present company stimulating and perhaps amusing. Only now she knew better. Days ago she'd set out to be wild, to be flamboyant, to be independent--except she'd only managed to make a sad muddle of everything.

Oh yes, she could easily slip into the fashion she thought she'd wanted; all she had to do was turn to Lord Quinn with a hint of encouragement and she knew she'd be swallowed up into his universe. Or if not him, then any of a dozen other gentlemen would do for a casual affair, or a rash debauchery, or any other kind of folly. She could join Lisette in her venture into the ancient rituals, the herb craft, the witch-like worship of nature. She could dance, and flirt, and be as forthcoming as she'd been as a child... Only she now knew she didn't want to be or do any of those things.

What she'd really wanted, underneath the long weight and frustration of her mourning, was happiness. Simple, unfettered, uncomplicated happiness. Yes, she wanted admiration, but of the variety that wrapped around a person like a downy counterpane, constant and comforting and treasured. She wanted to know a man's affection, the kind that thrilled even as it protected, the kind that gave your heart a home even as it offered one in return. She didn't want sexual dalliances; she longed to be prized, to have a true bond with an honest soul. She wanted years, not moments.

And now, what she wanted most seemed the furthest from her reach.

Alone with her thoughts in a room full of people, she felt a veil of sadness fall over her, a cheerless supernatural shawl that made her part of and yet removed from the scene in which she sat. For a moment she'd touched such a man as the kind she dreamed of cherishing...and it had been she who'd turned him away today. The one that had made her realize the yearnings of her deepest heart, was the very one she'd done everything possible to repulse.

She looked up slowly, again becoming aware of where she was when she noted that the dozen-odd people had come to their feet and were calling for their cloaks. She'd been too lost to despair to know anything but relief that her guests were leaving at last, when Lord Quinn moved before her.

"Do you not go with them?" he asked, his eyes clearly hopeful she'd answer in the negative, so he might seize a moment alone with her.

She couldn't bear it with her heart so ragged and tattered in her breast. She was afraid of her own vulnerability, afraid of what she might say or promise him, out of sheer sadness. "Of course I go," she said at once, leaping to her feet though she'd not the faintest idea where the party proposed to venture.

With everyone bundled in coats and tumbled into one of three carriages, it was only as the party was descending upon a residence she didn't recognize, that her question of "Who lives here?" was answered: "Lord Ewald."

Olivia came from the coach slowly, only to stand frozen in place, beyond reluctant to enter this particular home. Her mind was decided for her when Lisette caught up her arm and pulled her forward, propelling her like an unruly puppy through the gate and to the front door. Someone had already knocked and was informing the butler that they wished to make a call.

They were issued into a morning room, standing about in groups until the butler returned to bow his master into the room.

Lord Ewald made the collective group a leg, and looked up with a questioning but calm glance around. "What is this then?"

"A traveling party," Lisette called, pulling Olivia forward with her.

There was that in the woman's stance which posed a dare, causing Olivia to cast Lord Ewald one desperate, beseeching look she hoped was taken as an apology before she was unable to make her eyes continuing meeting his at all.

"To where do we travel?"

Lisette gave a peal of laughter. "To here, of course! From Lady Stratton's. We demand food and drink and entertainment, do we not?" She turned to the crowd, lifting a hand to solicit confirmation.

"Aye!" "We do!" "Of course!" came the enthusiastic responses.

Ian hesitated, his hand jingling his watch fob as he considered. He looked at the gathering, but his eyes settled on Olivia, who steadfastly watched her hands crease the pleat that was of such interest on the arm cuff of her pelisse.

Finally he replied, "Yes, of course. We shall contrive something, shall we not?" He held up a finger. "I have one request, as tomorrow promises to be a tedious day for me, with reports and figures and other such necessities with my bankers. I request we end the evening by eleven, or, lacking an ending, you promise to move on to another host at that time."

There were groans, but after a few good-natured grumbles, it was agreed.

His home was invaded, with table surfaces ruthlessly deprived of their papers or bibelots as they were dragged from a variety of rooms to serve as card tables. Wine began to flow at once, still cool from the ascent out of the wine cellar. Whist was declared the game, the stakes fixed at a ha'penny a point, and a variety of chairs procured after the fashion of the tables. Various debates on how to assemble the teams went forth, but their host ended the discussion by insisting names must go into a hat, and he must draw his partner first. Heads were counted and it was seen they had one too many people for the sets.

"Allow me, please, not to play. Whist is not quite ze game for me," Miss Lyons offered at once.

Alexander gaped at her, silently suggesting he knew otherwise, but before he could say as much Miss Lyons placed a finger on his lips. "*Non*, Lord Hargood, I do not mind," she purred. "You need not be gallant by offering me your seat. Please, please, everyone, I insist you draw ze names now. It is decided, I shall sit out."

Ink was brought and slips of paper torn, and all the names were tossed into a hat. Lord Ewald reached in, unfolded the small paper, glanced at it very briefly, and declared, "My partner shall be Lady Stratton."

She blushed to the roots of her hair, but she moved to the chair he indicated by pulling it out for her, and murmured a very small "thank you" as he circled to sit on the opposite side of the table.

"I say," a young man named Lord Malley cried, "I just drew Lady Stratton's name as well." He held up his piece of paper with a puzzled look.

Ian turned in his chair, one arm hooked over the back, and replied, "It must have been written twice. My apologies, my lord. Draw again, and you'll see who your partner is in a trice."

Olivia flashed Ewald a look, only to lower her eyes until Lord Malley was paired with Miss Burridge.

Lord Quinn, with his partner, a Miss Sumner, was placed at the table next to Olivia's. He seated his partner so that his own seat was facing Olivia. His features were ordered, but his occasional glances spoke volumes about forgiveness, second chances, and a burning desire to speak with her, driving her to avoid glancing his way.

The first game went well, the other players being challenging enough that Olivia needed to concentrate on the play of the cards. This was complicated, for after the first hand, Ewald slid the score sheet to her and requested she keep score. Then he proceeded to ask after her brother and sister, and when that subject was quickly exhausted went on to inquire into her schedule for the next day. She murmured and shifted in her seat, and tried to think of an answer that admitted nothing that would reveal where and when he might find her, even as she tried to keep from throwing the cards at him and telling him to let her be so that she might think.

It was then she caught the gleam in his eye, and she knew by the smile that floated around his mouth that he was quite aware he was disturbing her composure--and suddenly it seemed quite absurd she'd allowed herself to become so flustered.

She found herself smiling at him, albeit reluctantly, and then, as her wits returned to her, nearly laughing in a wave of released aggravation. Just because they were in the same room (even though she'd never intended to come here tonight), and just because he'd made sure she was his partner (it was only a game of whist), it didn't mean she had to lock herself away in a dungeon. If she didn't desire a private moment with him, then she would simply see one never occurred. Simple. She'd managed with Lord Quinn so far tonight, hadn't she? Now she'd laugh at herself and go on with the evening as a rational person would.

She looked up at him again, now disappointed to find Lord Ewald's attention had left her. *Among other things, I am a perverse little creature, rejecting his attention only to turn about and crave it.*

He was gazing about the room, his brow knitting briefly, until one of his eyebrows shot up. Olivia couldn't help but look over her shoulder to see that Lisette had just reentered the room. The woman hesitated in the doorway, one hand springing to her throat as she found two sets of eyes on her, but a toss of her head apparently restored her equilibrium.

She crossed at once to Ian's side, lounging in the settee sitting off his elbow, in a fashion that made Olivia store the vision of the sheer elegance of how Miss Lyons reclined for some later use in her own life.

Across the room, Alexander scowled at the demonstration and Miss Lyons's nearness to Lord Ewald.

The lady looked up from under her lashes, and murmured to the latter. "How goes the play, my lord?"

"How do you find my home, *Mademoiselle*?" Ewald countered in a level tone, but the stare he directed at her was stony.

The woman didn't blink or even blush. She didn't answer either, but Olivia saw communication ricochet between her and Ewald, hard-edged, reminding her of the haughty face she'd seen when Miss Lyons was offering her prayer to the Earth Mother.

Ewald looked away first, to pull out his pocketwatch. "'Tis nearly eleven--"

Lisette stood up, clapping her hands to gain everyone's attention. "Lord Ewald's chef has kindly offered to serve us all a late-night repast. Please finish your play so zat we may dine!"

This was met with a round of cheers.

She turned back to Ian, a smile on her lips. "I know I have presumed, but ze chef, he assures me it will be no trouble. Some cold meat. Some bread. He says he only needs a few minutes to begin service."

Ian regarded her steadily, and finally said, "How can I disappoint my guests? Of course we must dine." Again their eyes met and held, and Olivia could feel the tension between them like a washing line stretched taut.

The mood was disrupted when Lord Quinn stood, announcing his table was done, and coins were exchanged to pay off losses. The other tables soon followed the pattern.

"Let us retire to the dining room," Lord Ewald said, extending his arm to Olivia.

The servants hurried in and out, caught in the unanticipated act of having to set a late-night supper. The bustle was contagious as china and crystal and silver were placed around them, so that conversation bubbled. Olivia was placed on Ewald's right, he at the head of his long table, and on her right was Captain Russell, whose rather unfashionably short hair nearly matched the color of his red military coat. He went on for some time about the defeat of the

French at Vittoria, which Olivia found quite interesting, even if it was a completely improper discourse at table and in mixed company.

When she turned to Lord Ewald, she couldn't help but recall the other night when he'd stayed to be sure she wasn't in over her head. How different this gathering from that, she sighed with relief. She could no longer deny she'd learned the reckless life was no life for her. Freedom was not the way to happiness; happiness was the way to freedom.

"You smile, my lady," Ian said.

"Do I?" she answered, extending the smile for his benefit. "I was remembering another midnight meal we shared."

He leaned forward. "I was remembering that, also."

She looked down at her plate of carved ham and egg tart, then up again, at the length of the table. "I beg your pardon for my being part of this troop of invaders."

"You're the only reason I tolerated the others' presence."

"My lord," she said, the words a tiny scold, but with little effect since she smiled.

"I only speak the truth." He spoke again, very softly, " *'L'amour vient de I'aveuglement, L'amitid, de la connaissance'.* "

She recognized the century-old quote: *Love comes from blindness, friendship from knowledge.* Her lips parted and she stared at him in wonder, for there was a glow in his eyes that spoke only to her. As she fought to find a response, he might have said more, except a servant approached and whispered in his ear.

He murmured an apology to her alone, rose, and slipped quietly from the room.

In but a few minutes, during which time Lord Ewald didn't return to table, Olivia saw the revelers put down their utensils and rise, forming into mixed groups, the gentlemen and ladies for once not breaking off into separate factions. For a few minutes, Olivia

174

joined a group admiring a pastoral painting over the mantelpiece, but just when she thought to move on, a hand touched her shoulder.

"Lady Stratton," Lord Quinn said down to her.

She turned to him, a bit chagrined she'd let down her guard. "My lord."

He took up her hand, settling it on his arm. He drew her a little aside, and she let him because it was not so far as to unduly alarm her.

"I know this is a most inauspicious time, but I find I can no longer wait to speak my mind," he said softly. "You must know I am all that is anxious to hear you say you will be mine." He overrode any comment she might have made. "You cannot pretend you didn't know I felt this way."

She shook her head, admitting as much.

He went on again. "You understand a little of how important my position is here in England. I feel you are one of the few women who would be willing to support my efforts, one of the few to understand what very important work I do. You know the Druidic rites I practice have been a part of England for eons. I tell you now, a very necessary part. There are such things as ley lines, magic, karma, these terms we mortals use for the supernatural. I believe it has been given unto me to keep the faith and practice and power of the Druids alive. It's by keeping their magic active that I keep England alive. I am convinced that Rome became so unmindful of its roots and its need to have its religious leaders practice the arts, that she allowed her magic and power and majesty to crumble and wither, and therefore that mighty nation was made small. This must not happen to our England. Indeed, Goddess willing, it will not so long as I live."

He was so very sincere, so very full of faith, she could only take him seriously. "How did you come to receive this charge?" she asked, her words kind if not convinced.

He blinked once, then twice. "Why, I was simply born with the talent. As I grew and read and learned, I recognized my destiny."

"I see."

"But that's just it! You do see. You are charming, and delightful, and everything a man could want. Especially a man such as myself, who could not abide condemnation, or stupidity, or mulishness. I need someone who will not only allow, but perhaps even one day encourage my work. I know you are such a one. I sensed the magic happening that night at the masquerade. I know it now by every utterance you make. Your honesty is essential, your hypocrisy nonexistent, your--"

"My lord, you're mistaken," she interrupted him with a gentle sigh. "I'm afraid I'm thoroughly dishonest, if that this is how you see me."

"I can't believe it! You judge yourself too harshly, I think--"

"Not at all. I stand here, letting you propose to me, and all the while my affections lie in another direction." Her heart suddenly raced. *I said it aloud.*

She watched Quinn's face fall.

"I cannot promise you anything, not when I care for another," she said.

Lord Quinn shook his head at her words, crestfallen before her.

She recovered herself and smiled sympathetically at him. "I have come to know you a little, my lord, and hope to cherish a friendship with you. But it is because of that friendship I tell you now, I do not love you."

"Love," he tried to smile in return, "is not necessary, not at first. We have attraction, I dare to believe. If we married, love would come, given time."

"No," she shook her head softly. "It cannot come when it has been given elsewhere."

"You speak of Ewald," he said sadly. He watched as she gave a tiny nod. "I should have known by the way he held you, by the way you let him hold you."

"I should have known, too." She put her hand on Lord Quinn's arm. "But there are obstacles there, too, my lord. Pray speak to no one of my affection toward him. I...I am far from sure of him." She stopped to swallow down further words that mingled anxiety and hope. "It seems to me these matters of the heart are too oft beyond our control, and almost always completely illogical. Let me say only this: I would not have been much of a helpmeet to you, for I find all this Druidism rather shocking."

"You wouldn't, not in time," he said, one corner of his mouth raising half hopefully that she'd reconsider.

She just looked at him, eyes brushed with an apologetic empathy for the disappointment in his face.

He sighed heavily. "I do appreciate your honesty. It means much to me, for it means you are my friend, despite it all. I do not make friends lightly," he said, taking up her hand to press it between his two.

"Then I count myself fortunate to be called such."

"Ah, Olivia, will you not just think about it for a while?"

"I am so sorry, but no."

His shoulders drooped. "I hope you'll understand if I choose to leave..." he looked around at the other partygoers, "this gathering early?"

"Of course. My lord, just so you know, I was very flattered by your offer. As will another lady will be, when you find her."

He straightened his shoulders and spoke in his more usual fashion. "Now, that was meant to remind me there are other fish in the sea, so I stand reminded."

"May I ask you something then?"

"Of course. My friends may ask me anything."

She went up on tiptoe to whisper in his ear. "I find I must know. Do you, as a group ever...that is to say...disrobe together?"

He gave her a bittersweet smile, then perhaps almost laughed. "I'm afraid now you'll never know. You had your chance, and it is gone."

She sighed, and his assumed smile widened, and then he bowed himself out of her presence.

# Chapter 18

Ian waited in his unlighted library. There was a shuttered lantern hidden under his desk, but the thin cracks where a tiny bit of light showed were turned from the door, and otherwise did nothing to relieve the gloom. If any of his guests came in, they would hopefully flee the dark and the chill, the latter of which was beginning to make Ian wish he'd thought to bring his cloak. Nor could he check his pocketwatch to see the exact time, but it must surely be half past eleven or better by now. He looked, again, to the library door, where only Kellogg knew to find him, but it remained stubbornly unopened.

*Where in Hades is Douzain?* Or, for that matter, the agents Sir Terrence had this morning assured Ian would find the stupid, fleeing man to drag him back here.

Indeed, *had* the French informer fled? Or had he been carried away by someone working for the French? Ian frowned, unconvinced some person or persons had slipped unnoted in and out of his home to seize Douzain, but hating the idea he might have failed in his task. Douzain's would-be identity papers, now out of the locked drawer, though few, weighed heavily in Ian's coat pocket.

There was a scratching sound at the window, so that Ian stood up straight, listening, peering. A man pressed behind the shrub outside and close to the glass, eyes darting to see into the dark room. Ian's shoulders relaxed even as he watched the man jerk with shock at seeing Ian step forward.

He worked quickly to unlock and push the window open. Georges Douzain thrust in his head, looked around again, and finally slipped a leg over the casing. A moment later the entire man had tumbled, bag, cloak, and all, not very quietly, through the window. The man lay on the floor for a moment, and Ian caught a small sound of caustic speech, decidedly French.

"It's me," Ian whispered to the man, identifying himself in the dark, "Viscount Ewald." He fetched the lantern and raised the sliding panel, letting a small pool of light include them both.

The Frenchman scuttled to his feet, and combed back his hair with both hands, his bag resettling against his back by its strap over his shoulder. "I 'ope you understand zat I am trusting you, my lord *vicomte*," the Frenchman said in a breathy whisper back.

Ian lifted an eyebrow. "And that's why you ran from my home?"

Douzain drew himself up, looking a brave man before a firing squad. "Tell me true, is Mademoiselle Lyons 'ere, or now being called to your 'ouse? 'Ave I put my neck back in ze noose?"

"Lisette Lyons?" Ian asked, confused for a moment, but then his eyes widened. "She's an agent? Would she report your presence here to someone?"

"You told me you know 'er, and zat is when I wonder if I am in a trap? So I leave. But I know nothing. 'Ow am I to leave England? What path is zere for me to follow? So I must come back to you."

"With scarce time to spare, *monsieur*," Ian said sharply. "You are to sail tonight. We must leave at once--"

"*Mon cher vicomte*, I must know. If I am to be taken by zis woman tonight and 'er," he struggled to find an English word, but settled on, "*gendarmes*, I wish to know now. I beg you. Just to know before I am taken--"

"Through no deed of mine will anyone take or harm you," Ian interrupted, letting his insult show. He reached into his coat pocket and withdrew the papers Sir Terrence had carried to him this morning. "These papers give you your new life, *monsieur*."

Douzain held his breath and stared into Ian's face. When finally he reached out for the papers, his hands trembled, and perhaps even more when he saw they were indeed documents granting him a new existence.

"*Merci, merci,*" the man crooned, stepping to hold the papers near the lantern. "'Randolph Ralston, American.' *Mon Dieu,* so I am now an American. Who would believe this, eh?"

"Over there, everyone. It is a land of many accents. You will not be the first who has helped us who has been located there."

"It is said in France zat ze escaped ones, we are always sent to Scotland. I never zink of America."

"I am informed that's what we wish everyone to think," Ian replied. "Especially the French."

Georges folded the papers and secured them in a buttoned pocket inside his dark cloak. "I 'ave said it before, *monsieur*, but I most truly zank you. Please forgive my doubts."

"Then it's time for us to leave. I have a carriage waiting, on the hope you'd not gone for good."

"But your guests--? I hear zem and I zink again, per'aps it is not safe 'ere? Per'aps I am right to run? But I look in the windows, and I choose to make the gamble on you-- "

"My guests are all the more reason to leave at once, before they think to miss me."

The words were not even quite out of his mouth when the door opened, revealing a begowned figure. Lisette Lyons closed the door behind herself and stepped into the small circle of light, staring directly at Georges.

He gasped in horror, casting a wild-eyed look at Ian. "So! I am betrayed?"

"No," Ian said at once. He stepped closer to Lisette, mouth tight with anger. "I know what you are now."

She drew back a little, and cast Douzain a dark look.

"You were clever to associate with Lord Quinn. Being among his strange group diverted attention from your oddities of behavior."

"I know," she answered.

Georges looked from one to the other, drawing back a tiny step at a time, as though he would flee out the window once he achieved just enough distance.

"But you are too late. You must also know there is nothing you can do now," Ian said flatly. "I am escorting Douzain out of the country, now."

Her eyes were hard and glittering, and for a moment the three made a frozen tableau, held in place by doubt and tension. Finally, with uncanny calm, she nodded her head in agreement. "I suppose it is true. I cannot stop you from whisking *Monsieur* Douzain from our reach, at least for now. You will simply see zat I am restrained, zat I may not contact my allies, while you run to ze north. So, I must allow this little fish to go free--zat I might also escape."

She reached up, seizing the seam between her bodice and sleeve, and wrenched it. It ripped and sagged forward as she reached to run both hands through her hair. Pins went flying, and tendrils of golden-brown hair fell around her shoulders. She then slapped herself across the mouth with the back of her hand, and her appearance of ravishment was complete. She turned, as the stunned men stared at her, and fled from the room, her growing wails reaching their ears from the hallway.

"*Merde,*" Georges swore.

Ian reached for the other man's shoulder, shoving him toward the door. "Hurry!"

They hadn't even reached the front door when Lisette stumbled into the hall, a circle of wide-eyed witnesses behind her. She raised her hand, her long finger pointing accusingly. "Ze viscount, he did zis to me!"

Ian's heart plummeted as he saw a shock-faced Olivia standing among the others, staring at him. "Of course I did not," he said as calmly as he could, again pushing Douzain toward the door.

"Oh *oui*, deny it, fiend!" Lisette sobbed, bringing her fisted hands to her forehead, weeping into her arms so artfully that Sarah Siddons would have been impressed by her acting, as certainly were a number of the guests.

A young man, Mr. Hayden, stepped forward, hands slowly curling into fists as he frowned at Ian. "You did this to Miss Lyons?"

Lord Quinn came behind everyone, observing the scene silently, narrowing his eyes as he slipped forward and took a wide-eyed Douzain by the arm, preventing him from slipping out the door.

Ian was struck dumb, for he saw at once how clever she'd been. *Who was the Viscount Ewald anyway,* Hayden and others might be thinking. Hadn't he spent a great deal of time in heathen lands? Wasn't he the outsider? Was it possible he'd done this terrible thing? And then, of course, Lisette could wail and slip away, under proclamations of her need to be gone from the scene--in order to warn her confederates, while he himself was made to answer to her charges. Douzain's escape would fail, for the man had no idea what ship, of the tens if not hundreds at the docks, to meet.

Ian made his decision after only two beats, even though he wished by all that was holy that Lady Stratton was gone from this scene.

"*Mademoiselle,*" he said to Lisette, his face as stiff as his shoulders. "I deny I touched you, but harm has been done you. You must allow me the opportunity to amend this grievance. Please say you will do me the honor of becoming my wife, by accompanying me at this very moment to Gretna Green. My good friend, Mr. Douzain, will accompany us."

The crowd gasped, and Douzain tried to break away from Lord Quinn, with no luck. He gave a little squeak of discomfort. The crowd rustled, gazes leaping from person to person, following the contretemps. Ian kept his gaze toward Lisette, but he would have sworn one of those gasps had belonged to Olivia. His heart fell, knowing what she must be thinking, assuming.

Lisette's tears had been erased in a moment, and her eyes narrowed at Ian. She must be thinking he meant to take Douzain to Scotland; that the man would escape under her very nose.

Her hand whipped out, gathering up Olivia's with a pinching grip. She tugged Olivia forward. "And Lady Stratton will be my chaperone, to be sure you carry out zis marriage and do not attack me again." She did not smile, although there was a malicious triumph in her eyes at her countermove.

Ian stepped forward, his hands closing into fists, well aware at once of Lisette's scheme. She'd not picked Olivia randomly; she'd chosen the one person who would keep him in line. She knew he'd do nothing to endanger Olivia.

"Miss Lyons--" he growled, only to be interrupted.

"I will go." It was Olivia, speaking words in direct conflict with the abhorrence marking her features.

His heart slipped further south.

Olivia's brother, Lord Hargood, burst through the crowd, his face bright red. "My sister's not going anywhere, with any gentlemen, without me along!" He glared at them all, but lastly at Lisette, his eyes filled with doubt and with flickers of insult and injury.

Ian took in a deep breath, accepting what was unfolding. "Then let us away, at once, I insist. I have some money in my library, and that will have to suffice for us all." He stepped past Lisette, not offering her his arm, his boot heels beating a staccato as he went through the parting crowd, toward his library. Lord Quinn must have released Douzain, for the man scurried to follow Ian. Lisette trailed, her hand still locked on Olivia's arm.

It was the work of a moment for Ian to seize up a purse and a bag from his library desk, and then he led them out the front door. His eyes met Olivia's over the slightly shorter Lisette's head, and for a moment he was frozen again. What could she think, with him standing there with an already packed bag? He couldn't blame her if she thought this whole event had been staged.

The other guests all went to find their outer garments.

"Quickly," Ian said, wanting to drive away before the others came out to find their own carriages; they might only complicate an already messy situation. Fortunately, Miss Lyons seemed of like mind, giving Lord Hargood a push in the back to urge him to follow Georges Douzain within the coach.

Lord Quinn stepped forward, towering over Lisette and Olivia, his eyes only on the latter. "I will come as well," he stated darkly.

"Zere is no room," Lisette snapped.

"There isn't," Ian admitted.

Quinn threw Lisette a poisonous look, then fixed on Olivia again. "Miss Lyons is probably not what she seems. You mustn't trust her with anything. Lady Stratton, it's my fault you're in this position, and I insist--"

Brows raised in shock at the pronouncement, Olivia had looked to Ian, who'd shaken his head firmly behind Quinn's back; clearly he meant her to know the situation needed no further complications. "Thank you, my lord, but no," she said. "My brother will see that all is well with me."

Quinn meant to protest, but she pushed past him, this time leading with Lisette being dragged along.

Ian followed them into the coach, rising up to speak to the driver, telling him to drive away at once. The coach leaped forward almost before he could climb inside, leaving an deeply scowling Lord Quinn behind.

***

Olivia was seated next to Lisette inside the darkened carriage, facing backwards. On the other side of the carriage the three men crowded together. No one spoke. Olivia liked the quiet and the dark, because then she could think without having to work hard to avoid anyone's gaze.

She was as conflicted as she'd ever been. She couldn't figure it out: why had Ian offered for Miss Lyons? He'd not assaulted the woman, Olivia was convinced of that. There'd been the way he'd looked at her; a wealth of information had been contained in that sharp, quick, anguished glance--and it had been clear to her he'd not done it. He was chagrined to be put in the position in which he'd been placed, but it was somehow unavoidable. And dread--she'd seen fear in his eyes. Fear that she wouldn't understand, wouldn't trust him to explain it all later.

Well, she didn't fully understand why he'd done it, but that wasn't why she'd agreed to come. She'd agreed because she knew, all at once, that it was the only way to have any possible ability to make sure such a marriage never took place. Something was terribly wrong here, and she'd do all she could to prevent it from becoming a worsened situation. Ian had won that right from her when he'd stepped forward, fists clenched, trying to protect her from whatever Miss Lyons had thrust her into the middle of.

And who had she looked to when she'd needed another opinion? Not Lord Quinn, but Lord Ewald. He'd shaken his head, disallowing Quinn's added presence in the coach, and she'd accepted his counsel without question. She'd trusted him.

How many times had she trusted him, or turned to him, or relied on him, just in a few weeks's time? And now again, even though her brother was not three feet from her, it was Lord Ewald's lead she looked to.

Something in her middle separated from alarm and worry and upset, and floated up to make her lips form a soft smile, her eyes widen in the dark the better to read the man's face, and, impossibly, made her want to laugh aloud.

In the darkness of the carriage her foot slipped forward, until it bumped into Ian's boot. It was not the right time, for they'd not exchanged the kind of words that reflected her buoyant manner, but nonetheless she needed to tell him something of how she was feeling. She lifted her slipper, letting it tap three times on the leather over his toes, then lowered it next to his.

There was a hesitation, and then, to her joy, he slipped his boot over her slippered foot and lightly tapped three times in return.

Of a sudden they had no need of words, each suddenly and preposterously euphoric in the midst of a dark, uncertain flight into the night.

# Chapter 19

Quinn arrived at his home five minutes after Lady Mackleby's ball was ended so abruptly by accusations of assault and an elopement. He was in a foul mood as he moved up the stairs to his front door. Olivia had refused him, however kindly, and again when she hadn't let him join her misbegotten party of five.

Lisette had put on quite the performance. Over the past few months, he'd increasingly felt he was being used by the woman, and so had used her in return: to serve as his hostess, to utilize her undoubted talents to the purpose of uncovering those souls like his own who wished more for England than present day religions offered; and, for a brief while, her body. That had not lasted long, and he ought to have known his heart might be foolish, but it had seen what his mind would not. Still, his distrust had grown, and this past week he'd been paying a Bow Street Runner to learn more of the lady.

His butler met him at the door. "My lord, there is a man who wishes to speak with you."

Quinn knew from the butler's tone that it was not a person of refinement. "Where is he?" he growled.

"I put him in the yellow salon, my lord."

It was the Runner. He handed Quinn an envelope with a broken wax seal.

"She's a French spy, m'lord," said the investigator, pointing to the pages Quinn unfolded. "And there's the truth of it. I took it away from the bloke what she paid to carry it. 'E's got a nasty bump and a visit to gaol to show for his trouble. And there's my report. I've a mate what can make a sure thing of any code, even from the French like that. This here only took him about twenty minutes to figure."

Lord Quinn noted the missive written in Lisette's hand, and read through the decoded report, noting the attention to detail. The rumored or reported location of English battalions; a list of who was subject to extortion and how to enact such, including one high-ranking member of the War Office; a list of those who could possibly be persuaded to the French cause--she was exact and observant, and condemned by her own hand.

And Olivia was caught in her traitorous company.

Quinn folded the information together with tense hands, and reached for a purse of coins. "Allow me to extend my thanks along with this payment. This information will be given to those who have some power to stop such acts of treason. You've served your country well."

"Right-o," said the man, pinching his fingers to his hat brim in a salute before he slipped from the house.

Lord Quinn stood quite still after the man was gone, his sour mood having shifted to fury. He'd nursed that worm, that creature who would do all she might to pull down his beloved England. He'd sponsored her, despite his growing suspicions, had made it possible for her to settle exactly in the crowd that made her treacherous business so much easier to conduct.

He closed his eyes, reaching out with his senses to feel his home. He lifted his arms and let his fingers reach for the ever-present tingle of magic. And there it was: a disruption.

So, worse yet, he'd made it possible for the treacherous vermin to unbalance the magical ley lines that overlaid this property. The proof of his conclusion was immediate: Olivia had said she'd not have him. That never would have happened if the magic had been whole and unstained by the very poison he had nursed at this, his home, his altar, his world's hub.

Now he had to correct the error. Olivia was in love with another man, but she'd said that, just as their relationship had not been permitted to blossom, neither might this other with Lord Ewald. He, Richard Quinn, could put all the cosmic misalignments back into balance by bringing her nothing less than her heart's desire. Only that would allow him to undo the damage his association with Lisette had caused.

How had he ever let Olivia go off with the very creature who threatened her happiness, who would damage the future of the greatest nation on earth? Even though the idea of truly surrendering hope of her to another made his heart hang all the more heavily in his chest, he couldn't let anything happen, couldn't let Lisette come between the destinies of Olivia and Lord Ewald; he shuddered to think what would happen if she succeeded.

He strode from the room, calling for the return of the carriage that had just been sent to the stables.

# Chapter 20

They'd been in the carriage long enough their eyes could make out more in the dark now. As soon as Lisette realized Douzain had a bag, she seized it and dug through its contents.

"No weapon," she assessed with disdain after a thorough search with both hands.

"It is too much," Douzain grumbled.

Ian made no reply, lost in his own thoughts. He didn't know how it had happened, but by some wonderment Olivia had refused to accept the worst of him. It must have somehow, miraculously, become clear to her there was more to him, to this interplay with Lisette, and she'd not retreated from it. Had in fact reached out to him, easing the wailing of his soul by a few simple taps in the darkness. Hope had been reborn from that simple acknowledging caress and the understanding carried with it. She didn't care if he had a secret. He pledged, God willing, that not another day would go by where they didn't speak, didn't clear up the past, didn't get beyond what had once been. He would see to that, regardless of Lisette or Douzain or anyone else in this world.

When Douzain's comment solicited no response, the Frenchman went on, "I object to 'er going through my bag, but, more so, that you do zis for me, my lord. To marry her"--he pointed at Lisette with disgust--"it is 'orrible. I feel the great guilt zat zis should 'appen."

Ian merely shrugged.

Alexander cleared his throat. After having cast a great deal of scornful silence in his until-recent lover's direction, now he joined in the commentary. "I object to this elopement as well. I mean to tell you, Lisette, I cannot help but feel you might have had something to do with your own...er...manhandling."

She didn't answer him except to give a click with her tongue and a disdainful sneer. Suddenly sitting forward, she cried out, "Why do we slow down?"

"Because we have arrived at our destination," Ian stated. He turned to Douzain, reaching into his coat and handing the Frenchman a purse of money. "*Monsieur*, this is where we part. I was told your ship is the barque at the far end of this dock, the *Providence*."

"Ship!" Lisette cried, her eyes darting to the window, her hands flying to her skirts as she acknowledged the truth of what she saw at the window with a French curse. A lamp marking the beginning of the dock lent more light by which she affirmed their location.

Douzain took Ian's offering and his bag, and nodded to him. The Frenchman started to rise to slip out the coach door, only to pull up short when he saw Lisette had extracted a small pistol from a pocket in her skirt and leveled it at him.

Olivia gasped, and Alexander cried out in disbelief, "Lisette!"

"Lord Ewald, you almost out-witted me. I admit I zought we were hurrying toward Scotland."

"Not tonight," he said dryly.

She made a hissing sound, and the pistol stayed leveled at Douzain. "You are going nowhere," she told him.

"I didn't think of a pocket," Ian commented, the glint of his eyes far more dangerous than his pleasant tone. "And I thought there was at least a chance you might sacrifice Douzain against the hope of marrying me," he mused.

194

"We both know zat was never more zan a ruse," Lisette snapped. "But I will allow you to take me to my associates." Her eyes darted to Douzain. "Me and zis traitor." To him, she said, "How could you trade your knowledge of troop movements to ze English? For mere money? How can you play so false against your homeland?"

"Ze 'omeland zat never paid me for ze information--?" Douzain began to argue back, but Ian spoke over them both.

"*Mademoiselle*, tell me, how long can you be utterly vigilant? How long until you look away just for a moment? Before one of us tries to disarm you? You've not been so clever as you imagine. Give me the pistol, and I guarantee you will be treated gently until I hand you over to the Home Office."

The word "until" hung between them in the carriage. Ian saw the gleam of metal that was the pistol, the hard line that was Lisette's mouth, and Olivia's bright, anxious eyes taking in everything.

"Eventually something will happen," Ian insisted. "I will try to take the pistol. Or Douzain will leap from the carriage. A struggle is inevitable."

Lisette raised her arm, bringing the pistol to shoulder level. "Zen I might as well shoot him," she said. "And I will shoot you, and zis woman and her *stupide* brother." Lord Hargood blew out an indignant breath. "You are all spies, so my country will be happy enough to know I have disposed of you."

"Olivia? How do you figure her to be a spy?" Ian said at once, stalling automatically as he weighed the chances of lunging for the pistol.

"I saw you go together into zat shed, at the masquerade. I had her followed afterward, and learned zat the 'Cat' was Lady Stratton."

Olivia only nodded confirmation. Hargood didn't startle, so he'd known too, but he gave his sister a sideways glance of disapproval anyway.

"Ah. So you knew zis about her already, Lord Ewald. You only prove me correct to be suspicious of ze woman."

"You could not have seen much at the masquerade, or else you would have known Lady Stratton and myself were hardly conducting affairs of state," he drawled.

Alexander came half out of the squabs at the implication of intimacies, until the pistol swung his way. For her part, Olivia may have blushed, but there was nothing apologetic in her gaze as she murmured a protest for her brother's sake.

Ian kept his eyes trained on Lisette and the pistol. "Should we choose to overpower you, you know you cannot kill us all. Think! Your career is finished, whether we live or die. You are no good as a spy for France now; too many people know who traveled with us in this carriage. If you are not found dead among us, they will know who the murderess is. There are too many witnesses about. The sailors waiting on the tide--"

Her snarl stopped his words, as did the answering glint in her eyes. She spoke softly. "Zose things are all true, my lord. Zerefore I will have to make a different manner of escape, and I can only do zat if I take a hostage." She turned the pistol on Olivia.

Ian started forward, but a hard glare from Lisette stopped him. "You know I will kill her. All of you, climb down at once."

The men exchanged glances.

"Now!" Lisette screamed, the sound echoing in the small space.

Douzain reached for the door, but before he descended he looked at Lisette and hissed, "*Vache!*"

"*Bastard!*" she hissed back.

Alexander gave a parting shot, too. "To think I held you in my arms!" He spat on the carriage floor at her feet. Ian remained seated, not moving.

"Get out," she said, making a quick flicking motion with the pistol toward the carriage door, the lamplight through the open door letting them see a small muscle in her jaw working.

"I would make you a much better hostage," he pleaded.

"You would not. You, a spy, always knew and accepted the danger. But if zis one is as innocent as you claim, zen you will not risk her taking harm. And even if she is entirely guilty, still I know I am far more safe with her, for to send *gendarmes* after me is to send death after her, I promise you. Now, no more talking, no more delays. Get out."

His jaw tightened as his whole body tensed, but then his eyes focused on the pistol's muzzle. *Can I push it aside? I could take the bullet, so long as Olivia is not hit... But if all goes ill...*

"I will come after you, you know that," he ground out, even as he reluctantly rose.

"Go," was Lisette's only reply.

Olivia's hand shot out, touching his own. Lisette made a warning noise in her throat. His fingers wrapped around Olivia's hand, squeezing three times, hard. His eyes were full of anguish and dark promises of revenge for this moment. His voice was deadly as he told Lisette, "Heaven help you if she's harmed."

He released Olivia's hand and, once outside, suddenly checked, his body stiffening. He cried out, "Olivia, get down!" even as he flung himself back into the doorway, pushing her down and into the side panel as he tried to cover her with his own body.

A flash of light illuminated the inside of the carriage, momentarily making everything entirely clear and colorful, but it faded in a heartbeat. The loud crack that had accompanied it, however, lingered in the ears. Still, even with ears ringing, Ian heard the pistol in Lisette's hand fall with a heavy clunk to the floor.

He moved off Olivia, scrambling up into the coach, his foot connecting with the hard metal of the pistol. He didn't hesitate, kicking it from the carriage. He went into a half crouch in the limited space, facing Lisette, ready for attack.

The woman looked up slowly, the light of the lamp having been brought nearer; it showed where her hand came away bloody from her right shoulder. "I'm shot!" she gasped.

"And soon to be hanged," Lord Quinn assured her, pushing his face past Ian to look within the coach, Lisette's pistol now in one hand, the dock's lamp in the other.

"Lord Quinn!" Olivia cried.

Ian reached out two hands to gather Olivia's in his own. As Quinn backed up, Ian climbed down from the carriage, never letting go of her hands, and hurried her away from the bleeding woman. Quinn leveled Lisette's pistol at her where she sat white-faced, assuring she stayed where she was.

The minute Olivia's feet touched the ground, Ian pulled her into his embrace. She melted into him, letting her hands clasp him hard about the ribs. He pulled back, just enough to take her face in his hands, hands that trembled just a little. "When I had no choice but to climb down and leave you with her...!" he ground out.

For an answer she slipped her arms around his neck, and he hugged her so tightly she was forced to go up on tiptoe.

At length he set her back, reaching into his pocket for a handkerchief. "You've blood on your face. I don't want that creature's blood on you a moment longer," he said, applying the handkerchief to her brow, nose, and left cheek, "as we know it is quite poisonous."

She reached up, her hands clasping his wrists as he tenderly wiped her face.

People had come, summoned by the sound of a pistol shot and a woman's wailing as Lisette was wrestled from the coach by Hargood. The initial red blossom on her gown now had added terrible stripes all down her front. Several explanations had to be given to the new arrivals before Hargood was given Quinn's kerchief for binding Lisette's hands together. Olivia's brother followed as two chosen sailors dragged a weakly struggling Lisette to one of the ships and its surgeon's attentions.

At length Ian wrenched his eyes from Olivia's face to look at Lord Quinn. "Thank you for your timely arrival, my lord. How is it you happened to come after us, and so well prepared?"

"You were easy enough to follow. You told your coachdriver to wave his whip and act the fool?"

Ian nodded. "I wasn't sure he heard my whisper after I told him aloud to be away at once. I didn't know if anyone would report us or follow, but I'm sincerely glad you did."

"It worked, for he was noticed. I was able to see you must be making for the docks, not toward Scotland at all." He looked to Olivia, but spoke to Ian. "I'm only glad you also had the wit to pull Lady Stratton out of the line of fire."

Ian's arm slipped around Olivia's waist.

Quinn put down the lamp at their feet, and reached to his pocket to produce the papers the Bow Street Runner had brought him. "I give you proof of the vile creature's traitorous activities. I know you can get them into the right hands. Justice must be had. For England, of course." He looked down at Olivia in Ian's embrace, with a chagrined uplifting of one corner of his mouth. "And for my friend, Lady Stratton."

She stretching out her hand to him. "Thank you. Thank you so much, my lord."

Lord Quinn made her a bow, then closed his eyes and took in a deep breath. "I can feel it, can you not?" he asked of no one in particular as he opened his eyes again. "The rightness of it all--I do believe the cosmos is pleased with today's work. Fine work, indeed."

A distant scream echoed off the Thames. Quinn shook his head as if annoyed. "I feel I must be sure the creature doesn't bleed to death before she faces judgment, so I would consult with the surgeon. Ewald, will you take Lady Stratton home?"

"Of course." Ian offered Quinn a deep bow, which was returned in kind before the man headed down the dock to the ship's gangplank, leaving the lamp at Ian and Olivia's feet.

Douzain came forward then, his bag of belongings in his left hand to free him to use his right in a quick bow. "*Mon cher vicomte*, I zank you again, but now I flee to my ship."

"Yes, you must go, and may good fortune travel with you. I wish I could say I'm sorry I didn't meet you at the masquerade, but," he looked down at Olivia, "I'm not."

"*Oui*, my lord," Douzain replied. "I suppose I can understand zis." He made a flourish of a bow as an additional thank you before he hurried away.

***

As the soon-to-be former Frenchman made his way toward freedom, Olivia gave a hiccupy kind of laugh, perhaps as much from released nerves as from relief no one beyond Lisette was harmed. Still holding her to his side, Ian let the blood-stained kerchief he'd wiped her face with drop to the ground. He began to lower his head, as though to claim a kiss, but she pulled back a little.

"And here we are again, kissing in the dark."

He seemed to consider for a moment. "I cannot think of a more pleasurable pastime, unless of course it is kissing you in the light of day."

He did kiss her then, regardless of the time.

When Ian pulled his mouth away at last, a cheer from staring seamen greeted them, causing them both to flush and laugh. "It seems I've compromised you," he said.

Olivia's eyes darkened and a shadow of doubt crossed her features. "I compromised you first. That night. You need not feel beholden to...to anything just because I was such a terrible flirt and-_"

"No," he said firmly.

"No?" she repeated. She began to pull away, her face coloring, but he caught her hands, pulling her up fast against his chest.

"Olivia, I'll have no more holding back. I weary of you feeling you must make apologies for meeting with me in the dark that night. It started everything."

Caution left her face, and she almost smiled. "In the dark. Where we kiss." She got no further, for he kissed her again, melting any lasting doubts away.

When at last he pulled away, he said, "My dear lady, I know it is a rushed thing...but I think we both know we've found something with each other. I know it's far too early. I know it's impossible. But say you'll agree to marry me anyway."

She'd wanted to be daring, to be alive and experiencing what that meant. However, some would say she'd be a fool to give up what she'd dreamed of for so long, and all for too-new kisses and unfounded hopes. It *was* too soon, too impossible.

But she didn't hesitate a moment longer. "Oh yes," she breathed, and accepted the pledging kiss she'd hoped to gain by her answer.

When he let her go, she laughed. "I'm afraid my answer has one small contingency attached, though."

He lifted a brow.

"My maid is my guardian dragon. You will have to pass muster with Mary Kate. Only then am I free to marry you."

He looked astonished for a moment, but then he managed a half-bow without ever letting her go. "I will even answer to servants, if that is your requirement, my lady," he said, perhaps not realizing she maybe meant it more than one could expect. But Mary Kate would want her mistress to wed soon, in order that her lady might settle down to proper domesticity--and with anyone but the highly questionable Lord Quinn.

Suddenly Olivia was laughing, and Ian with her, until he pulled her even closer and kissed her all over again.

"Really now, that's quite enough of that," Hargood's voice floated to their ears as he and Lord Quinn approached, their evening clothes spotted with Lisette's blood. Ian turned toward them, reluctantly at last releasing her.

"How is *Mademoiselle* Lyons?" Ian asked.

"Seems likely to survive," Lord Quinn said, mouth turning down. "She's tied to the surgeon's table, guarded by a Marine, and a constable has been sent for." He changed the subject abruptly. "Ewald, I insist on being best man." A resigned smile hovered near his mouth.

"He's offered? You've accepted Ewald?" Hargood said to his sister, eyes going wide.

She colored prettily. "Yes."

Ian replied to Quinn. "I'm afraid that duty falls to my brother, if we can arrange it around his duty. But I would be honored if you'd stand up with us as well."

Quinn did his best to look pleased, nodded acceptance, then took Hargood by the upper arm. "Come, fellow, me must let these two remove from this sorry scene."

"But I can't leave my sister alone--"

Quinn spoke in a stage whisper. "Can't you feel the magic going on here? I sensed some of it on All Hallow's Eve, but I'm afraid I misinterpreted it in my favor. Alas, we've no part of it, you or I."

He led a yet reluctant Hargood back toward the ship.

"He's very odd, but I like him very much," Olivia said, smiling up as Ian handed her up into the coach, on the forward-facing seat not covered in blood.

"Surprisingly, so do I."

"He seems to believe we started some magic at the masquerade."

He grinned. "I believe it, too. So you see you've no choice. You had to answer yes to me this night. It was fate."

"For England's sake," she nodded sagely, then grinned.

"Yes, for England's sake," he smiled into her eyes, which softened at the tender look in his as he added in a whispered voice, "but mostly for my own."

He closed the coach door as she smiled radiantly at him, the evening rapping around a woman just reborn to a reason for living, loving, and laughing, and a man who'd at last found a home for his heart.

# ABOUT THE AUTHOR

Teresa DesJardien lives in the Pacific Northwest with her husband, grown children, and growing grandkids. She's been a financial and a file clerk, a mommy, a page, a bookseller, a very young and hot grandma, and an author.

Website:   teresadesjardien.com
Twitter: twitter.com/TDesJardien
Facebook:  facebook.com/teresa.desjardien.7

63677201R00114

Made in the USA
Charleston, SC
11 November 2016